L

Rample And the Silver Screen

Lady Rample Mysteries:
Book Three

Shéa MacLeod

Lady Rample and the Silver Screen
Lady Rample Mysteries: Book Three

Printed in the United States of America.

Cover Art by Amanda Kelsey of Razzle Dazzle Designs
Editing by Alin Silverwood
Formatting by PyperPress

To A

With Love

Chapter 1

"Ophelia, we must pack at once!" Aunt Butty charged into my bedroom waving a piece of paper in the air. Her hat—a pink straw cloche with a wide brim and an enormous matching pink bow tacked down with giant red cherries—was slightly askew and her face flushed with the exertion of charging up the stairs of my London townhouse.

My maid, Maddie, stared at me with wide eyes over the mound of clothing currently piled in the center of my bed. She clutched a handful of lacy knickers to her narrow chest as if they might protect her from my aunt's exuberance.

"Did you leave the front door unlocked again?" I asked Maddie from my place on the chaise longue—China blue to match the wallpaper of my bedroom—where I'd been directing her activities.

She shot me an outraged look and went back to neatly folding a silk slip before tucking it into a yellow suitcase. "No, m'lady. I locked it proper."

Which meant my aunt had, no doubt, used her key. The one I'd given her for emergency situations only. I highly doubted this was such an emergency.

"Aunt Butty, darling," I said with infinite patience, "what does it look like I'm doing?" Was my aunt losing her marbles? Surely not. She was far too young, just tipping sixty.

Aunt Butty stopped and stared at the disaster that was my bedroom as I waved my hand toward the pile of clothing and my startled maid. My aunt squinted as if unsure what to make of the open trunk and the pile of hat boxes stacked haphazardly in the corner.

"If you recall, we spoke about needing an adventure. A trip to the South of France. My villa?" My late husband, Lord Rample, had left me very nearly all his worldly possessions—including a very nice house on the French Riviera. The only thing he hadn't left me was his title, entailed, and the manor house in the wilds of Yorkshire. Both of those had gone to his ghastly cousin Binky. Frankly, I was happy to see the back of both of them.

"Dearest Ophelia," Aunt Butty said, plopping down in a chair after removing the dresses Maddie had draped across it, "I am well aware of our plans. I haven't yet taken leave of my senses. In fact, I've already sent Mr. Singh ahead to prepare the villa, as you well know." Mr. Singh was Aunt Butty's Sikh butler. She'd met him during her travels and apparently hired him on the spot. Typical of Aunt Butty, but Mr. Singh had proved a treasure and could be relied on to accomplish whatever task was set before him with dignity and thoroughness. "No, my dear, I have a much better adventure in mind." She held out the paper to me.

With some trepidation, I stared at the black, scrolling letters barely able to make them out. It appeared to be an invitation of some kind. "Who is this Cyrius Bimbo?" I asked.

"Cyril Brumble," she corrected, propping her elbow on my vanity and managed to knock over three bottles of nail varnish in the process. Maddie dumped my knickers back on the bed and rushed to save my cosmetics.

"Bimbo. Brumble. Whatever the case may be, who is he?" I handed back the letter.

"Cyril Brumble is a very dear friend of mine," she said. "We met many years ago in New York. You see, he was putting on a play—as one does—and I was invited to the after-party. That's what they call it in show business. Everyone was three sheets, and this naked woman—"

"Aunt Butty," I interrupted, "please! I don't need to hear about naked ladies and New York. Who is Cyril Brumble?"

"Oh, yes. He is one of the foremost producers of films in Hollywood."

I felt a little flutter of excitement which I quickly quashed. I was inordinately fond of moving pictures, especially those involving dashing private detectives or rugged cowboys. Still, it wouldn't do to seem overeager. "Interesting. And what does he want with you?"

"As you can see by the letter, he wishes me to attend his nuptials in Hollywood, California next month."

"Oh, yes?" I plucked the letter out of her hand and squinted at it. There it was. The words "marriage" and the date, August 25, 1932. "Are you going?" I felt a pang of disappointment. I'd have enjoyed her company in France. The time I didn't spend with Hale Davis—my… paramour, for lack of a better term—that is.

"Yes. And I want you to come with me."

My jaw hit the carpet. "You realize that's a ten-day trip. One way." It would be simply ages before I got to my villa. Then again, Hollywood! Swimming pools! Movie stars! I was nearly giddy at the thought. But I had plans. Important ones.

"Eight, if one hustles," Aunt Butty said, not batting an eyelash at the logistics of such an undertaking.

"Still much longer than going to the French Riviera." And no Hale. He was a jazz musician and was set to perform at a club in Paris for the next few days before heading to another gig in Nice. My plan was to meet him there away from the prying eyes of upper crust English society. In France, no one would care that I was a rich, white widow or that Hale was a poor, black musician. And an American to boot! We could finally spend some real time together instead of sneaking moments here and there. And perhaps I could finally decide what I wanted this thing between us to be. What it *could* be. If anything.

"Buck up, Ophelia," Aunt Butty snapped. "There's adventure to be had. It's *Hollywood*." As if that clinched matters.

Images of glamorous parties, handsome film stars, and free-flowing champagne flitted through my mind. It did sound divine. We'd only be gone... two weeks or so for travel each way, a couple of weeks for the wedding... yes, I could surely make it to Nice by the end of September. I'd still catch Hale there. We wouldn't have as much time as I'd hoped, but still... there'd be plenty if we made the most of it.

"Yes," I said at last. "I think it's a marvelous idea, darling."

"Excellent. I already have the tickets." Aunty Butty shoved herself to her feet. "We leave in the morning. Maddie's to come, too."

And she sailed out of the room, leaving Maddie and myself staring after her with our mouths open.

"Well, I never," Maddie finally managed.

"You took the words right out of my mouth."

"You're going *where*?" Chaz demanded as he poured me a glass of champagne. It fizzed up to the top, a few stray bubbles sliding over the rim.

I'd decided that such an adventure required a celebration and there was no one I'd rather celebrate with than my best friend, Chaz. And there was nowhere I'd rather celebrate than the newest jazz club in London, Grande Café. It had sprung up shortly after the downfall of the Astoria Club after the owner was convicted of murder. Something I may or may not have taken part in. The conviction, I mean, not the murder.

While the Grande Café wasn't quite as posh as the Astoria had been, it was still very upscale with mirrored walls behind the live band, flocked purple wallpaper, and a marble-topped bar that served more varieties of cocktails than even I knew what to do with. The band was playing a lively tune I didn't recognize, but which had my feet tapping to the beat, and the dance floor was packed with men in dark suits and women in flashy evening dresses all the colors of the rainbow.

"Hollywood, darling," I shouted over the din. "Isn't it a scream? Don't tell Aunt Butty, but I can't wait! Too bad I can't stuff you in my suitcase, but we've been invited to a wedding. Hardly the done thing to drag you along, more's the pity."

Chaz languidly blew a smoke ring at the ceiling. "You know, an old school chum of mine lives in Hollywood now. Archie's been simply begging me to come visit for ages. Now seems as good a time as any." He winked.

I very nearly squealed in joy but settled for clapping my hands instead. "Really? That would be *brilliant.* We could see the sights together. Check out the clubs. I bet they have an amazing music scene. You're brilliant!" I lifted my glass in a toast.

"Of course, I am," he said with a knowing smirk that turned him from dashingly good-looking to devilishly dreamy. It was really too bad he preferred the company of men. He would have made an excellent suitor. Not that I had any intention of marrying again—I quite liked having my freedom—but still. "It's settled then. I've got a couple things to take care of here, but I'll book the next available boat across the Pond. Be there before you know it."

"This will be an adventure," I declared, topping off my glass. "To Hollywood!"

Chapter 2

I felt like an absolute bumpkin, but I couldn't help myself. I sat in the back seat of the Bentley with a silk scarf wrapped over my hair and stared about me like a young farm girl in the big city for the first time. There were *palm trees*! Oh, sure, they had them in the French Riviera, but I'd only ever been there once. And these were tall, spindly, soaring things—so different from anything I'd seen before.

Behind us came a much older car carrying Maddie along with the bulk of our luggage. Aunt Butty had debated bringing her maid, but the girl wasn't well-trained, so she sent Flora off to join Mr. Singh at my villa. I felt rather sorry for him. Flora could be… challenging.

The cars wound up and up through the narrow streets of what our driver had referred to as "Beverly Hills." Every now and then, I caught a peek-a-boo glimpse of sea blue through the trees and hills. The Pacific Ocean, far off in the distance, sparkling in the sun. Breathtaking.

I'd asked if we would be close to the sea, but the driver had given me a startled look and assured me that only poor people lived down near the beach. The wealthy and important lived up in the hills. I considered that utter nonsense, but who was I to tell the Hollywood elite how to live? Still, I was determined to visit the ocean before I left California.

I'd hoped we'd be able to sail with Chaz, but he'd been forced to stay in London another day before catching his own ship west. It was a pity. It would have been a great deal of fun to have him along. As it was, the voyage was entirely uneventful.

The trip from London had taken nine days in all. Nearly six on the steamer over the Atlantic, and a further three on the train cross-country after Aunt Butty hustled me directly from the port to the station without a moment to enjoy New York City. We'd been collected at the Los Angeles train station by a uniformed chauffeur with a brand-new Bentley in a rather attractive shade of green. He'd had the top down, "For the view," he'd explained. And despite feeling overly warm, dusty, and out of sorts, I'd been wide-eyed the entire ride.

At last, we pulled into a long drive that wound among the trees and shrubbery, reminding me of the manor houses in England. And finally, the house came into view like something out of *Grimm's Fairytales* complete with turret. With its white-washed walls and dark timbers, it looked like a Bavarian castle!

"Cyril always did love to make a statement," Aunt Butty said, leaning forward to get a better look. "At least with his surroundings. Poor man."

I frowned. "What do you mean?"

"You'll see."

The car swept up the drive and came to a stop at the front door. The chauffeur—who'd earlier introduced himself as Sam—hopped out and opened first Aunt Butty's door, then mine. "Go on in," he said. "I'll bring up the rest of the luggage once it arrives."

He had dirty blond hair beneath his driver's cap and an oddly flat accent. Almost, but not quite, nasally. His skin was sun-kissed—no surprise in this land of harsh sunlight—and his eyes the precise color of the ocean I'd glimpsed on the drive up. He was ridiculously handsome and clearly knew it. I swear he flexed his biceps as he strode toward the boot of the car.

Trunk, I reminded myself. I was, after all, in America now.

America! The stuff of dreams! Home of the silver screen. Probably, being a member of the aristocracy, sort of, I shouldn't be so overwhelmed. But honestly, it was too, too thrilling. Aunt Butty had assured me we'd be seeing movie stars everywhere. I was secretly hoping to meet Gary Cooper. The man was positively swoon-worthy. I'd thought so ever since I'd first seen him in *The Virginian.*

"Where is that Cyril?" Aunt Butty muttered, joining me. "He'd better have a drink ready for me." She charged up the two shallow steps and into the house, with me trailing behind, gawking at everything like the country girl I had once been. London, after all, hadn't always been my home. I'd grown up in the small Cotswolds village of Chipping Poggs. Every now and then I still forgot my sophisticated veneer.

The inside of the mansion was dim and cool, a relief from the heat outside. The entryway soared two stories high with a stairwell sweeping elegantly upward directly in front of the door. The floor was dark hardwood polished within an inch of its life, pink rugs scattered across it for a spot of color. A rococo table against one wall held an enormous arrangement of pink roses.

"Butty! My darling!" A man appeared at the end of the hall and rushed toward us with arms outstretched. He was short, perhaps an inch or two shorter than me, slightly built with narrow shoulders, a receding hairline, and a thin moustache. He wore light beige trousers and a white button-down shirt and looked to be perhaps mid-forties or so, though there wasn't a gray hair in sight. No doubt due to liberal application of hair dye.

I instantly knew what Aunt Butty had meant. There was nothing extraordinary or interesting about Cyril Brumble's appearance. Perhaps that was why he enjoyed his surrounding to be so over the top.

"Cyril, you old dog," Aunt Butty crowed. They embraced, kissed each other's cheeks, and embraced again. It was all very ebullient. My aunt is rather more prone to dramatics than the usual English person. She turned to me. "This is my niece, Ophelia. Lady Rample. Ophelia, this is Cyril Brumble, a dear friend of mine from way back."

"Not too far back, Butty," Cyril said with a laugh before greeting me with equal warmth. What he lacked in physical attributes, he made up for in personality. "Welcome, Lady Rample. Welcome to Hollywood. And to my home." I noticed he had a very slight accent. German, if I wasn't mistaken.

"Please, call me Ophelia." I figured since we were in America and they didn't have titles, I might as well blend in.

"And I am Cyril. Naturally." He clapped his hands, delighted. "Now, if you will follow me, I have drinks!"

I would have liked to wash up first, but drinks were a necessity, and there was no way on this green Earth I was going to be able to keep my aunt from her libations.

"This is the living room," Cyril announced as we passed through the doorway at the end of the hall from whence he'd come. "Just finished decorating it. What do you think?"

"Very striking, Cyril." Aunt Butty's tone was one of approval.

It was a large room with high ceilings, heavy wood beams, wide plank floors, and a stone fireplace large enough to roast a small cow. Plush, comfortable-looking chairs and sofas were sprinkled about—pink, like the rugs in the front entrance and modern in style and design. Heavy pink velvet drapes graced the long windows—pulled back so one could partake in the view of the lush gardens outside. An enormous art deco chandelier hung from the center of the room. But the truly startling thing was the mural painting on the ceiling itself. It portrayed a medieval scene—horses, huntsmen, knights, and so on—all in a hodge podge of color. It was... amazing. That's the only word I could muster.

"How've you been, Butty?" Cyril led us to a side board loaded down with liquor bottles.

"Can't complain," she said airily. "I've got my health. What more can one ask?"

"You English and your stiff upper lips. It is my opinion one could as very much more. Don't you think?

Vieux Carré for the ladies," he announced cheerfully, without waiting for a reply, as he vigorously shook an already-full silver shaker before pouring amber liquid into cocktail glasses and graced each with a lemon peel.

"Delightful!" Aunt Butty snatched one of the glasses from him and downed it almost in one go. Cyril didn't seem to mind, simply poured her another.

I decided to enjoy my cocktail and took it and myself to one of the plush armchairs. It was so dashed comfortable, I might never get up.

We chatted inanely for a bit. How was the voyage, did visit anyone in New York, and so on.

"Where's your bride-to-be, Cyril? I'm dying to meet her," Aunt Butty asked after a she'd polished off her second cocktail.

"Ah, Lola is out on a shopping spree," he said. "Darling girl. Trying to finish all those last-minute details so important to brides-to-be."

"You must tell us how you proposed. I'm all agog," Aunt Butty said, accepting another refill from Cyril before taking a seat across from me and crossing her ankles neatly. "Knowing you, I'm certain it was romantic." She turned to me. "When we were in New York, he fell for a showgirl. Took her up on the roof of the theater for a midnight picnic. Isn't that lovely?"

"Lovely," I agreed, taking another sip.

"So tell us about your proposal. Was it romantic?" Aunt Butty urged.

"Oh, it was." He got a dreamy look in his eye.

"Wait, wait." Aunt Butty held up one beringed hand. "First, how did you meet?"

"Oh, now that is a story," he said with a grin. Filling his own glass, he took a seat next to Aunt Butty. "We met at one of those Hollywood parties… you know the thing. Actresses and actors everywhere. All the movers and shakers. She'd just finished a film. I'd seen it and thought she was sensational. In any case, we struck up a conversation."

"As you do," Aunt Butty said over the rim of her glass.

"Indeed." He took a sip of his drink. "We became friends, you see. She's a marvelous actress, Lola, but she wasn't being taken seriously. So I thought I would help her out. Lend a hand. I knew once she got in front of the right people with the right parts, she'd really shine."

"And clearly she has," I said. "Even in England, we've heard of Lola Burns." She was one of the Hollywood darlings, star of the silver screen. The Golden Girl. A true blonde bombshell. How a man like Cyril Brumble had snared himself a beauty like her was beyond me. Then again, I don't suppose looks are everything, and Cyril seemed a nice man. Besides, there's something to be said for the sex appeal of power, though it certainly wasn't working on me. He reminded me of a dotty uncle.

"Yes, she's done rather well." He beamed proudly. "It was just friendship at first, but one thing led to another and, well, here we are!"

"And the proposal?" Aunt Butty prodded.

"Oh, now that was a thing—"

But he didn't finish his story. There was an almighty crash from the entry hall and an angry female voice yelled, "Cyril!"

Cyril blanched. "Oh, dear. I wonder what's gone wrong."

"Cyril!" The female voice held a sharp edge, and the sound of heels furiously tapping across the hardwood floor was unmistakable. Quick, determined steps. The steps of a woman not to be messed about with.

"In here, my darling," Cyril called out. He gave us a tight smile, a small tic flickering at the corner of his left eye. "You must forgive Lola. She's doing a new film, you see. Plus getting ready for the wedding. I'm afraid she's been rather... overwrought of late."

The clip clop of heels neared the living room door. The strident, nasal voice—nothing like the melodious tones from Lola's movies—continued, "Cyril, you have *got* to have a word with these people. This is positively unacceptable— Oh!"

Lola Burns stood in the doorway. I wondered if she realized she'd posed in the perfect place to show off her beauty or if it just came to her naturally. But she stood there, framed by dark wood, a ray of sunshine turning her hair into a halo of white gold. One of the most breathtaking women I'd ever laid eyes on.

She was a tiny thing, barely above five feet, but substantial where it counted—yes, I'm speaking of her bust. Her face was delicate and heart-shaped with a dimple in her chin, a beauty mark—probably fake—on her left cheek, and perfectly penciled half-moon brows. All the rage these days. Her platinum blonde hair was done in the most fashionable waves, and she wore her signature true-red cream lip rouge. I'd bought it at Harrod's one day, but it made me look like a tart. On Lola, it was sophisticated and elegant.

"Well, who have we here?" she asked with a small smile before striding slowly toward her husband-to-be, hips swaying side to side. I wasn't so mesmerized as not to realize her voice had changed the minute she realized she had an audience other than Cyril. Gone was the strident, unattractive nasal voice that sounded more like a gun mol than a starlet. She now spoke in the musical tones she was known for. She must have one doozy of a vocal coach.

"Darling," Cyril greeted her, rising to give her a peck on the cheek. "This is my dear *old* friend, *Lady* Lucas, and her niece, *Lady* Rample."

It escaped neither me, nor my aunt that Cyril had put an emphasis on the word "old." Granted, he'd also emphasized our titles.

"Aces! Proper ladies from England. That's swell! Dear Cyril has told me so much about you!" Lola rushed to greet each of us in a flurry of cheek kisses and perfume. It was floral with a touch of spice. I remembered reading in a magazine that Lola preferred Mitsouko by Guerlain. I found it a little heavy for my taste.

"Lovely to meet you, Miss Burns," I said with all the gravity of my station. "Thank you for inviting us into your home."

"Oh, that was all Cyril's doing, but you are most welcome." Her expression exuded warmth, but her eyes were carefully blank. As if she were playing the part of hostess in one of her movies. Just another role with the appropriate script to follow.

I was having a hard time deciding whether I disliked Lola or was drawn to her. Maybe a little of both. Either way, I had a feeling that I'd only caught glimmer of the real Lola Burns in the hall. Or perhaps that was a role, too.

"Now, my dear, have a cocktail and tell me why you are so upset," Cyril said soothingly as he rose to fix her a drink. She immediately took his seat, and I noticed once again, the sun high lit her hair and features perfectly. As if she knew exactly where to sit or stand in order to get the best lighting. I could take lessons from her.

"Remember that part in *Valiant Lover* you had me read for?" she asked, crossing her legs at the knee in an unladylike fashion and swinging one foot back and forth.

"Of course, my darling. You'd be perfect for it." He handed her a drink. Unlike the amber Vieaux Carré, this was a lime color. I wondered what it was.

"Well, they gave it to some b... Somebody else."

"That's impossible!" Cyril assured her. "I spoke to—" He seemed to catch himself and cleared his throat. "Who got it?"

"Katharine Hepburn," Lola spat. "Can you believe? She's not nearly as pretty as me. Nor as talented."

I would agree on the pretty. Katharine Hepburn was not pretty, but she was stunning, and she had *presence*. As to talent, Ms. Hepburn had more in her pinky than Lola would ever possess, but it wouldn't do to tell our temperamental hostess that. Something her intended clearly understood, for he commiserated with her, refilling her cocktail glass, reassuring her of both her attractiveness and her talent. Although I noted he behaved in a more fatherly manner than a lover.

"I will speak to my friend at the studio. I'm certain we'll get to the bottom of this," Cyril assured her.

For her part, Lola was quickly zozzled, her ranting becoming ever more unintelligible as she muttered about Cyril's friends. The way she said "friends" set my suspicions on high alert. Cyril finally excused himself and escorted her to her room. No doubt to sleep off the effects of both her temper tantrum and her overindulgence.

"Goodness me," Aunt Butty said when they'd at last exited the room.

I glanced over to find her shaking her head. "She's a bit... dramatic, isn't she?"

"It's not only that. It's that she's so... *young*."

"Yes, there is quite a bit of age difference, isn't there?"

"Twenty-three years!"

"There was more than that between Felix and me," I pointed out. When I'd married Lord Rample, I hadn't yet turned thirty and he was sixty. Large age differences between spouses weren't that uncommon.

"Yes, but that was different. You were quite mature, and both of you had an *agreement*."

It was true. Passion wasn't the stone upon which our marriage had been built. It had been friendship, companionship, and mutual admiration. He got an attractive young wife—if I do say so myself—and I got security. Marriages had been based on far less.

"Perhaps they have an arrangement as well," I suggested.

"Don't be daft. He clearly dotes on her. But I fear she's not *at all* suitable."

She had a point there. Despite my niggle of unease, he did seem to cater to her every whim. "Maybe she dotes on him, as well?" Even I could hear the doubt coloring my tone. As far as I could tell, Lola Burns was unlikely to be besotted with anyone but herself.

Aunt Butty snorted, her thinking clearly along the same lines. "I doubt that. What is she getting out of it, I wonder? It has to be something."

"He mentioned calling someone, a friend at the studio. When she was talking about the movie. Perhaps he's helping her with her career."

She sighed. "What a shame. He's such a nice man. So kind and generous to a fault. Why, do you know, one time he gave his coat—a very expensive one, too—to a beggar. In New York! In the winter! You haven't any idea how ghastly New York winters can be. He was a saint for doing it if you ask me. He deserves better than a gold digger."

Perhaps he did, but he certainly seemed happy enough with what he had. And I was pretty sure that Lola had plenty of money herself. I polished off my cocktail and got up to refill my glass. "I should probably check on Maddie. And I don't suppose Cyril would mind if I used his telephone, do you?"

She snorted. "You'd better reverse the charges. He may be rich as Croesus, but he's tight. That German thriftiness, I suppose."

So that explained the accent. "But you met him in New York, not Germany?" Aunt Butty had traveled most of the known world and had collected interesting acquaintances everywhere she went.

"Oh, yes. He came to New York as a young man. Got involved in the theater. Directing and whatnot. We met through a mutual friend at that party I mentioned."

"Yes," I said dryly. "The one with the naked woman."

She chuckled. "Indeed. Then he convinced me to play Titania in *A Midsummer Night's Dream."*

"*You were in a play*? On Broadway?" I asked, astonished. Why this surprised me, I couldn't say. Aunt Butty was full of tales of adventure. She'd do anything she took a fancy to. She once told me she joined a Buddhist monastery for a week because she liked the outfits. I had my doubts as to the veracity of her claim on that one.

"Yes, dear. For a short while. Marvelous good fun. Eventually Cyril gave up the theater and joined the movie business. Worked for some studio or other in New York before everyone moved out here to film in orange groves."

We'd passed some of those orange groves on the way from the train station. It was all so... exotic.

Something crashed overhead. The sound of breaking glass followed by an angry shriek.

"Movie stars," Aunt Butty sighed. "So overly dramatic."

She was one to talk.

Since Cyril didn't seem to be in a hurry to return to his guests, I decided to explore the main floor. And hopefully find a telephone. Aunt Butty chose to remain behind and enjoy another cocktail. I had no idea where Maddie had got to. One could only hope someone had shown her—and the luggage—to our rooms.

Stepping out into the hall, I turned right. The hallway dead ended at a simple wood door with a black knob. I opened the door and popped my head in. It was a cloak room, of sorts. Not the euphemistic cloak room of the English—cloak room being a code name for the toilet—but an actual cloak room with coats and wraps and hats hanging from pegs along the wall, boots lined up neatly by the door, and a bench for sitting on. Probably to put on said boots, though why anyone needed boots in this land of eternal sunshine was beyond me. Within the room there was a door straight ahead and one to my left.

The straight-ahead door opened onto a flagstone patio with a marvelous, kidney-shaped pool. Deck chairs, bistro tables, and potted plants graced the patio around the pool, creating an almost second living room. Thick foliage surrounded the whole thing, ensuring a private sanctuary.

Next, I tried the door on the left, which proved to lead into a thoroughly modern kitchen complete with brand new refrigerator, an electric range, and what looked like a dishwasher! Goodness, my kitchen at home seemed hopelessly out of date. I made a mental note to look into getting some new appliances. It would certainly make Maddie's job easier. She'd no doubt be thrilled as it would allow her more time lurking in my library.

A heavyset woman with skin the color of a copper coin and gray-streaked dark hair done up in a blue kerchief was kneading dough, occasionally smacking it against the kitchen table as if it had offended her. I quietly shut the door, not wanting to disturb her. She seemed... angry.

Back in the hall, the living room door stood open on my left. A few feet beyond, also to the left, was a second door, closed. Across the entry way on the right double doors leading to a dining room stood open, the room beyond done in heavy wood paneling and enough antiques to open a museum. Situated beneath the stairs was another door, discretely designed to look almost as if it were part of the wall. It led into what we British actually referred to as a cloak room. The neatly tiled room was all white with a small sink, toilet, and a mirror. After ensuring my hair and makeup were still presentable, I decided to try the closed door. I was betting it was a library. Or perhaps a study.

Sure enough, the room was clearly Cyril's study. His desk was surprisingly small. I had expected something large and extravagant and masculine. Instead it was delicately carved from pale wood, all curves and smooth lines. The top was glass and gleamed in the dim light reflecting back my image. It was so clean. Completely bare of the usual knickknacks and supplies so common in studies. Not even a pen marred the surface. Only a simple brass lamp with a green shade on one side, and a black telephone on the other.

I immediately sat down and placed a call. It would be late evening on the French Riviera, but I knew Mr. Singh would still be up. It took some time for the call to be routed, but at last a voice came on the other end of the line, tinny and full of static, but distinctly Mr. Singh.

"Villa de la Belle Mer." I could almost picture him in a purple *dastar,* his neatly trimmed black beard accentuating a face that was always calm regardless of my aunt's antics.

"Oh, Mr. Singh. It's Lady Rample."

"My lady, are you well?" His musically accented voice held a note of concern.

"Yes, yes," I assured him. "I'm fine. Aunt Butty is fine. I just... Mr. Singh. Could you possibly do me a little favor?"

"But, of course, my lady. Whatever you wish, I shall accomplish." He had one of those voices that just made one want to trust him. He also had the wherewithal to back up his promises. Mr. Singh had never let Aunt Butty down.

"Have you heard of a nightclub in Nice owned by an American? They play jazz music there, apparently."

"But of course. The Americana."

"You have heard of it then?"

"Everyone has heard of it, my lady. It is very popular at the moment," he assured me.

"Could you take a message to one of the musicians there?"

"Anything you wish, my lady." There was no indication from him of whether or not he approved. But of course, he was used to Aunt Butty's carryings on, so likely nothing I could do would shock him.

I quickly dictated a message. "The musician's name is Hale Davis. Please tell him that plans have changed, and I've been slightly delayed. He can visit the villa at any time and use the telephone to ring me here in Los Angeles." I quickly gave Mr. Singh the number, although I doubted Hale would use it. He was too poor to afford a call, and too proud to reverse the charges or leave me to pay them. It was frustrating to me, but I understood.

"Certainly, my lady. I shall deliver your message post haste."

Relieved that Hale would soon have my details, I hung up and made my way back to Aunt Butty in the living room. I found her snoring lightly, an empty glass sitting on the end table next to her. Apparently, the long trip, the heat, and the alcohol had done their work. She was out cold.

Cyril reappeared in the doorway. "Oh, dear. I am sorry. I hadn't meant to be away so long, but Lola... she's very delicate, you know."

"Yes," I murmured. "I could see that." I wasn't entirely sure I'd managed to keep the sarcasm out of my tone. Lola seemed about as delicate as a dandelion. "I'm afraid the travel has worn out my aunt." I waved my hand toward the sleeping Butty who let out a tremendous snorting snore.

Cyril repressed his merriment, but only just. "She would be appalled to be caught sleeping. I will have Sam carry her to her room."

"She'll be disappointed she missed that," I said. "She's always dreamed of having a handsome, well-muscled young man carrying her about."

"Don't we all, my dear!" I could hear Cyril's chuckle all the way down the hall.

Chapter 3

I found Cyril's comment... interesting. Did Lola know her husband-to-be found other men attractive? Not that I cared. Love is love, as far as I'm concerned. But it would be a scandal-and-a-half should word get out. It would probably ruin Cyril's career. Maybe Lola's, too. A blonde bombshell who couldn't keep a man? Unheard of!

Which might explain their hastily arranged marriage. Was Cyril trying to hide the truth behind a sham marriage the way so many did? Was Lola in on it? Or was the studio forcing this marriage on them in order to protect an asset? According to Aunt Butty, the studios practically ran not only Hollywood, but Los Angeles itself.

Still, I didn't have time to mull it over for long. Cyril and Lola were throwing an engagement party that evening down by the pool. I do enjoy a good party, but I'd hoped that since we'd only arrived that day, we'd be allowed to relax a bit before the festivities began. Apparently not.

Maddie had got out my Saxe-blue silk number from Chanel. She helped me slip it on and I immediately felt like the belle of the proverbial ball. Growing up, I'd never had such a magnificent gown, but Aunt Butty had introduced me to the world of designer couture.

The dress was sleeveless with a wide V-neck in the front and dipped to the waist in the back. The skirt was gored to flare from the knees, creating a fabulous sense of movement. And somehow, despite the fact it was mostly form fitting, it managed to make me look sleek and sophisticated rather than lumpy. Perhaps it was the full custom corset which sucked everything into place and smoothed the lumps and bumps. In any case, I did look rather fantastic, if I do say so myself.

Once dressed, I paused by the mirror to ensure my lipstick was in order and gasped in horror. "Maddie, what is this?" I whirled around and pointed to my chin where a giant, red pimple had appeared as if by some horrible dark magic.

Maddie squinted at my chin. "It's a spot, m'lady."

"But I'm…" I did a quick mental calculation. "But I'm thirty-five!"

"I'm aware, m'lady." Her tone was very dry, edging on sarcastic. Wench.

"But I am far too *old* to have spots!" That was something one left behind with the teenage years, surely.

She had the unmitigated gall to roll her eyes. "People of all ages get spots. Change in climate, no doubt."

"But what do I do? I can't go out looking like this." Not among the starlets and movers and shakers of Hollywood. Good, gosh! The very idea.

Typically, I'm not one to care much what other people think, but I was feeling a bit out of my element. Being forced to face Cyril's friends with an enormous spot on my face was giving me palpitations.

Maddie sighed heavily. "I'll figure something out."

"Quickly."

Another eye-roll. "Yes, m'lady. I think I can hide it." She grabbed a pot of vanishing cream and smoothed it over the spot. Next, she dabbed an ample amount of ivory foundation on it, followed by an inordinate amount of powder. "There." She waved toward the mirror.

Alas, the spot was still there! A giant lump upon my chin. But at least it wasn't an enormous red thing glaring at me. I sighed heavily. "It'll do."

She pursed her lips. "That it will, m'lady."

"Hopefully it's dark enough out there no one will notice." I had little hope of that since it was still light outside. Perhaps I could dally until the sun went down. But cocktails beckoned. And so did Aunt Butty.

We had adjoining rooms, identically decorated in the same pink as the rugs and furniture downstairs. I wondered it was Cyril or Lola that was so fond of pink. The wallpaper in both rooms was a pale pink with bouquets of blue roses scattered over it. The carpets covered the entire floor and were solid rose pink with insets of blue and yellow geometric patterns in the corners. Both bedroom sets were of carved walnut imported from France. Aunt Butty's featured an art deco thistle. Mine, a fan shape.

Aunt Butty's imperious knock on the connecting door summoned me forth, regardless of whether or not I was ready to face Cyril's guests. "Ophelia, stop dilly-dallying. We've a party to get to! If I miss Gary Cooper, I shall never forgive you." She'd all but swooned earlier when Cyril informed us the famous actor would be at the party.

"Coming, Aunt Butty."

I didn't bother with a handbag as I could always retire to my room if I needed to fix my hair or makeup. And it was still quite warm out, so I decided not to take a wrap, either.

Leaving Maddie to her own devices—which no doubt involved a romance novel pilfered from my library back home—I joined Aunt Butty in the hall. My aunt's eyes were sparkling with excitement. Her dress was also blue, but the similarities stopped there. Hers was a midnight blue, covered in sequins, and topped by a capelet in the same color. She wore a matching turban on her head—decorated with an enormous bejeweled peacock pin—from which poked a few artfully arranged gray curls. It was actually rather reserved for my aunt.

"Just think," she said, "we're going to meet movie stars!"

"Haven't you met all sorts of famous people?" I asked, surprised by her eagerness. Aunt Butty wasn't one to be swayed by fame or fortune. A handsome face, yes. Money or rank, not at all.

"Yes, but not *Hollywood* people. They're entirely different from Broadway people."

I had no idea what to say to that. I'd never met either kind of person, nor did I know what the difference was beyond the obvious stage versus screen.

The French doors in the living room had been opened wide, allowing guests to wander around the pool and gardens. Small tables draped with linens stood sentinel about the pool, graced with candles for atmosphere. A quartet played jazz music in one corner while black-and-white garbed servers circulated trays of drinks and hors d'oeuvres.

I helped myself to an amber-colored cocktail. One sip told me it was a Vieux Carré. Whiskey cocktail? I approve!

"Goodness," Aunt Butty murmured, "there must be over a hundred people here. However did he manage to fit them all in?"

"Ladies!" Cyril came toward us with his arms outstretched. He wore a red paisley smoking jacket over black dress trousers. Likely in an attempt to look relaxed and sophisticated. Instead he was flushed and sweaty. "Please, come. Let me introduce you to my friends."

He stopped at the first cluster of party goers and introduced us around. There was an older woman in a floral dress named Marie Dressler. She looked to be about sixty-something with a wide mouth and deep lines about her face. I hadn't heard of her, but everyone else treated her as if she were royalty, and Cyril informed us she was the top film star of the year which I found astonishing. Everyone in Hollywood seemed so… beautiful. Ridiculously so. Yet, here was Marie Dressler with her hefty frame, large nose, and booming laugh, the most popular of all of them. I liked her instantly and determined to see any of her movies that made their way to London.

There were a couple of other people whose names and faces I promptly forgot. Then there was a handsome, dark-haired young man who was called Wayne Palmer. He gave me a half smile, but all the time his attention was elsewhere as if he were looking for someone.

Cyril then led us around the pool toward another group of people—mostly men—who were laughing uproariously. In the center of the group, Lola stood, beaming upon her subjects. Clearly, she was a woman who enjoyed the spotlight. And she did it well in a cream-colored, bias-cut dress by Vionnet that showed off her lush figure to perfection.

"Oh, Cyril, there you are," she called. "Gary has just been telling me the most marvelous story about Frankie. You *must* hear it."

"She means the director Frank Borzage," Cyril murmured. "He just directed a film starring Cooper. *A Farewell to Arms*. I don't know why she insists on calling him Frankie. No one else does." He raised his voice, "Yes, my love. Coming. In a moment."

"Is that Gary Cooper?" I asked. There was a flutter somewhere in the region of my stomach. I guess my aunt wasn't the only one excited about movie stars.

"Oh, yes. I'll introduce you if you like," Cyril said.

"Oh, my," Aunt Butty murmured, "isn't he the bee's knees."

He was, rather. Far more ruggedly handsome than he was in the pictures. Which seemed impossible. I resisted the urge to fan myself.

"I'll be right back," Cyril assured us. Then he pushed through the gathered men to lean over Lola.

Neither Aunt Butty nor I paid him any mind. We were too busy watching Gary Cooper. Heavens above, the man was a looker! He was ridiculously tall—no doubt I'd only come to about his shoulder—with just the slightest wave to his brown hair and the most piercing blue eyes I'd ever seen. When he smiled, he did so with a slight quirk to his lips that no doubt sent female hearts everywhere to fluttering. I know it did mine. And, if Aunt Butty's reaction was anything to go by, hers did as well.

"We should go introduce ourselves," Aunt Butty suggested, tugging my arm. "No doubt Lola will be sending poor Cyril off to fetch her a drink or whatnot. Shall we?"

"And how!"

But before we could get through the crush of people to Cooper, he said something to Cyril and Lola, then disappeared through the crowd.

"Dash it all!" I wailed. "He's leaving."

"Surely not," Aunt Butty cried. "We just got here."

We scurried after him, while trying to appear as if we were just leisurely chasing a movie star. It was perhaps ridiculous, two women of an age hustling after some young buck. But what can you do? This was *Gary Cooper*. If nothing else, I could at least get his autograph. Or speak to him for a moment. Oh, the bragging rights it would get us back home.

We followed him through the grounds to a flight of narrow flagstone steps that led up to the front drive. I was out of breath as we reached the top, Aunt Butty puffing behind me. Alas, we were just in time to watch Cooper climb into a green Duesenberg and speed off down the drive in a cloud of dust and gravel.

"Damnation!" Aunt Butty said.

"Language, Aunt!"

"Oh, don't you language me, Ophelia," she snapped. "I've heard you utter worse."

She wasn't wrong.

"Well, there's nothing for it. Back to the party, I suppose. I imagine there are plenty more handsome men." She turned and made her way back down the steps.

"Too bad Chaz wasn't here," I murmured to myself. "He'd have been thrilled."

I paused for one last look at the back of the Duesenberg just disappearing around a bend, then turned to follow her. As I did, I caught movement out of the corner of my eye. With a frown, I focused on a thick clump of bushes. There. Something moved, and it wasn't the wind. Much too large for a bird.

Instead of heading back to the party, I walked toward the bushes, curiosity getting the better of me. But before I got there, someone stepped out of them. She—it was definitely a woman—turned and for just a moment I caught a glimpse of her face: pale, with wide eyes haunted by dark circles. Her expression was one of... I wasn't sure, but it made me uneasy. There was determination to it. But something darker, too.

She caught sight of me and let out a startled, "Oh!" Then she turned and ran, disappearing into the thick tree growth that surrounded the property.

"What the deuce?" I started to go after her, but it was no use. She moved like the wind, and I was in heels. I shook my head. Probably just a reporter trying to get something juicy for her gossip column.

As I worked my way back toward the party, I passed an open window. Sheer curtains covered it, so I couldn't see anything more than shadows beyond it. Not that I noticed much. I was more intent on grabbing another cocktail and having a chat with Aunt Butty. I would have walked right on past if not for the loud voices coming from behind that curtain.

"Don't lie to me!" That was definitely Cyril. I'd recognize his accent anywhere.

"It's not what you think." The tone was pleading, but the voice softer so I couldn't tell who it was. I crept closer to the window. Curiosity is my weakness, I'm not ashamed to admit.

"I'm not a fool, Carter. I know what I saw. I've had enough," Cyril snapped.

Ah, so it was the butler Cyril was arguing with. But what were they arguing about? It didn't sound like a typical squabble between employer and domestic. It sounded more… personal.

"Please, Cyril. Please! I don't—"

"Enough. I want you out of here."

My jaw dropped. Cyril was firing his butler? But why?

"I'll pack my bags immediately." Carter's tone was stiff.

Cyril sighed heavily. "No need for that. Just promise me you'll stop seeing him."

"I will, Cyril. I will. It's already done. I promise you'll…"

Whatever else he might have said was cut off as loud voices echoed from down the path. Eager not to be caught eavesdropping on my host, I eased out of the bushes and back onto the walkway as if nothing out of the ordinary had happened. Just as I turned to go, I noticed there was another lurker who'd been listening in on the conversation between Cyril and his butler. I couldn't have sworn to it as it was dark, but I was fairly certain it was Wayne Palmer. Dashed odd place for him to be hanging about. And what was with everyone hiding in bushes tonight?

I continued on my way, mind a jumble of disjointed thoughts. There had been something about that argument that left me feeling very uneasy. If only I could put my finger on it.

I shook my head, dislodging my maudlin thoughts. It was a simple argument, that was all. It wasn't like they were threatening to kill each other. I laughed at my overwrought imagination and went to find Aunt Butty.

I rejoined the party and helped myself to another cocktail. But I couldn't quite forget the woman, or the expression on her face, nor could I quite put the argument out of my mind. Something cold settled in the pit of my stomach.

Chapter 4

"How would you ladies like a tour of the studio?" Cyril asked us the next morning. Despite having been up 'til all hours, he looked fresh as a daisy and twice as bright, dapperly dressed in a neat, light-gray suit which was much more attractive on him than the previous night's outfit.

"Sounds brilliant," I said, pouring myself a third cup of coffee. I might have overindulged just slightly. Those cocktails had been rather strong, and perhaps I hadn't had enough to eat what with the running after Gary Cooper. I forked another bite of eggs and toast and forced myself to eat despite the dangerous rumblings of my stomach.

"Oh, perhaps we can catch sight of that gorgeous Gary Cooper," Aunt Butty said, rubbing her hands together. "What a dish."

"Ah, unfortunately, he won't be at the studio today," Cyril apologized. "I did mean to introduce you last night, but—"

Aunt Butty waved a beringed hand. "No worries. What will be will be. No doubt we'll meet other interesting people during our time here." And by "interesting," I was fairly certain she meant handsome.

"Oh, certainly," Cyril said brightly. "William Powell, Boris Karloff, Myrna Loy... you never know who you'll run into!" He seemed as excited as we were, despite having worked among these people for years. "I plan to leave in an hour. Is that enough time for you ladies to get ready?"

"Of course!" Aunt Butty declared. She shoved back her half-eaten breakfast and hustled from the room like the Hounds of Hell were on her heels.

I finished at a more leisurely pace before making my own way to my room. It was only once I had Cyril's butler call for Maddie and the bedroom door was closed that I began my mad dash to get ready. I was done and downstairs with five minutes to spare. Possibly a world record.

The drive into Hollywood took a little over twenty minutes. Along the way, Cyril entertained us by pointing out the homes of various important denizens. Mostly, they were hidden from the road by thick foliage or impressive gates.

"While you're here, you'll have to visit Greystone Mansion," he informed us. "It's not far from here and is quite a stunner. Not to mention, it's supposedly haunted."

"How thrilling," Aunt Butty said. "We must put that on the itinerary, Ophelia."

After leaving the hills, we passed through acres of orange groves baking under the late summer sun. This late in the season, the trees were bare of fruit, but the leaves shone green and glossy and the deep shade beneath them beckoned.

Finally, we passed into Hollywood itself. Tall palms lined the streets and glowing white art deco buildings mixed with the richer earthy colors of hacienda-style abodes.

Cyril pulled up to a cream-colored building. An arc not unlike the Arc de Triomphe in Paris soared above us, braced on either side by elegant columns. Above the arch in stylish letters were the words Nonpareil Studios. Black wrought iron gates filled the arch, their graceful spikes formed by whimsical curls. Currently, they stood open, allowing Cyril to pull the automobile straight onto the large lot.

The tour was beyond anything I could have imagined. The studio wasn't just a single building; it was several buildings sprawled over what he referred to as a "lot." Frankly, it was more land than most English manor houses claimed these days.

He hustled us first through several massive warehouse-type buildings, each one dedicated to one thing or other. In the first, there was a painted backdrop made to look like the Pyramids of Giza looming in the distance. In front of that were set up massive pillars decorated with Egyptian hieroglyphs between which sat an elaborate gold throne. A couple of handsome young men—wearing next to nothing, their muscles oiled, and their eyes outlined in kohl—stood around with giant palm fronds in their hands and looks of boredom on their faces while men and women in street clothes rushed about shouting at each other.

"Goodness, me," Aunt Butty exclaimed, fanning herself. "What interesting costumes." I was fairly certain she wasn't staring at the costumes.

"They're filming a new picture," Cyril explained. "*Queen Nefertiti*. Should be delightful fun. Come this way. I'll show you a real wild west saloon."

Sure enough, the next warehouse was set up to look exactly like the interior of a saloon with a bar and everything. Cowboys with spurs and Stetsons lolled about, apparently waiting for their next scene.

Cyril led us from one "studio" to the next. Each one more interesting than the last. One was made up as a New York penthouse apartment. Another the courtyard of an Italian villa. And everywhere beautiful people in costumes of every country and era imaginable.

The most interesting place of all was what Cyril referred to as "the backlot." They'd literally built a city right in the middle of the studio! I could have sworn I was walking down a street in London. It was that convincing.

We even stopped to watch a scene being filmed. Cameras loomed over a man crossing the street. A car careened around a corner, narrowly missing the pedestrian. A woman shrieked. Someone yelled, "Cut!" And then there was a great bustling about.

I marveled at how similar the scene had been to an experience I'd had a few months ago. I repressed a shudder, reminding myself that the actor surely would not suffer the same fate as the man I'd seen nearly run over.

"It's all so thrilling!" Aunt Butty exclaimed.

"Isn't it?" Cyril's face shone like a child at Christmas. "Is it any wonder I left New York? Nothing beats Hollywood for excitement! This is where it's at, ladies. The future of moving pictures."

Somehow or other I got separated from Cyril and Aunt Butty. I didn't much mind. After all, the place was positively *crawling* with delicious men in the most divine costumes! Cowboys, centurions, tribal chieftains with feathers running down their bare backs. All oiled muscles and perfectly coiffed hair. It was any woman's dream come true. I wandered about a bit, happy to enjoy the rather delightful view.

At one point, I caught sight of a man dressed as a gangster. I was almost positive it was one of the men I'd seen at Cyril's party—Wayne Palmer. I opened my mouth to call out to him, but he disappeared around a corner.

"Hey, you there!"

I turned to find a middle-aged man in a gray suit standing a few feet away. While he was neatly turned out, he somehow made the suit look cheap and frumpy. He was about my height—five-foot-six-inches—and a bit on the plump side. He had the most enormous nose, thinning hair, a double chin, and a pair of wire-rimmed spectacles. And yet, for all that, those around him treated him as if he were the King of Siam, bowing and scraping and running around while he barked rudely at them. I disliked him as instantly as I'd liked Marie Dressler.

Whoever he was, I didn't much care for being yodeled at. So I gave him my haughtiest lady-of-the-manor look.

He strolled over, hands in pockets. "That's perfect! I like it. Who you with?"

"Pardon?" I asked in my most imperious tone. One that would have done the Queen herself proud.

"You with the studio? Never seen you before."

"I'm the guest of Cyril Brumble," I informed him.

"Great accent." He inspected me closely as if I were a prized horse. I was surprised he didn't pry open my mouth and inspect my teeth. "Not bad in the looks department."

"I say!"

"We should do a screen test."

A screen test? Me? Images of glamorous Hollywood parties and my name in lights danced through my head. Could it be that I would be the next Hollywood film star? Wouldn't that just make Lola burn. Ha!

"You'll have to lose some weight though."

I stared at him, aghast. "Well, I never." And I wacked him with my handbag right upside the head.

Chapter 5

"I still can't believe you bashed Louis B. Mayer with your handbag," Aunt Butty chortled as she added powder to her ample décolletage.

"I didn't know who he was," I said, eyeballing the spot on my chin in my compact mirror. Thank goodness it seemed to be fading. "And even if I had, the man is an utter jackanapes. Telling me I had to drop a few pounds. The cheek! Still, I hope I didn't get Cyril in trouble or anything."

"Pish posh. He'll be fine. Cyril can stand up to that man, you mark my words. Now hurry it along, Ophelia, dear. We've got a wedding to prepare for."

It was the next morning and we were gathered in Aunt Butty's room. Cyril and Lola had insisted we attend their wedding down at the courthouse. "A casual affair," Lola had assured me.

"Don't you think it's odd they're not marrying in a church?" I asked Aunt Butty as I dabbed on a bit of foundation cream in an attempt to cover the spot. It was fading, thank goodness, but it still stood out rather prominently. "You'd think what with Lola being a movie star she'd want something more... lavish… than a courthouse wedding."

"Neither of them is particularly religious," Aunt Butty said, "and I suppose they want to get it done and over with quickly. Lola starts filming a new movie in a few days. On location somewhere or other. I imagine they want to be married before that starts."

"I suppose. I just don't see the rush. Don't you think it's all a bit fast?"

Aunt Butty frowned as she powdered her neck with bergamot-scented French talc. "Yes, rather. It does concern me, I admit. I'm afraid this Lola may have ulterior motives. Still, Cyril is a grown man. One can hardly make his decisions for him, much as one might want to. I swear the world would be a better place if women ran it."

"True, darling. I suppose we must grit our teeth and enjoy the cake." I grinned.

Aunt Butty rolled her eyes. "Go get dressed. We're going to be late!"

In my room I donned the simple peach silk day dress with three-quarter flutter sleeves and a V-neck with a sailor bowtie. I paired it with cream heels and a matching handbag and beret.

Maddie eyed me approvingly. "You look lovely, m'lady."

"Thank you, Maddie. I couldn't do it without you. How are you getting on with Mr. Brumble's staff?"

She shrugged her boney shoulders. "That butler man, Carter, he's alright. A bit stiff. Mrs. Mendez, that's the woman wot cooks. She knows her stuff, but ain't got time for nonsense. Makes a mean sticky bun, though."

"High praise, indeed. What about Sam? The chauffeur?" The man was handsome enough to turn any girl's head, and I didn't want to lose my maid to some California Lothario.

"He's only got eyes for the Mrs."

"Mrs. Mendez?" I asked, aghast. I found it hard to imagine the angry middle-aged cook in a passionate embrace with the gorgeous young chauffeur.

"No, m'lady," Maddie giggled. "Wouldn't that be a sight? The mistress of the house. Lola Burns wots going to marry Mr. Cyril. He's besotted with her. Sam is, I mean."

"Well, who wouldn't be. She's stunning." Probably half the world was besotted with Lola.

She sniffed. "Stunning is as stunning does."

I lifted a brow. "What do you mean by that?" Though I knew exactly what she meant. And I didn't entirely disagree.

"Not very nice, is she," Maddie pointed out.

"She does seem rather temperamental, but we shouldn't say bad things about our hosts," I admonished. "Besides which, I suppose that's the Hollywood way. She's an artist. They're very high strung. Or so I hear."

Maddie snorted.

When I rejoined Aunt Butty downstairs, I struggled to keep a straight face. While her dress was similar to mine and in a simple shade of mint green, her choice of hat wear was... astonishing. It was tall, with a giant flower on the side, and shocking pink. I coughed delicately into my hand and tried not to catch her eye.

"Whatever is the matter with you, Ophelia?" Aunt Butty demanded. "Are you coming down with some vile American plague?"

"No, aunt. I'm fine. I see Marcel has outdone himself again."

She touched her hat proudly. "Ah, yes. He whipped this up for me especially for the wedding. Isn't he a gem?"

Marcel was her hat maker back in London. And apparently the man was either still living in 1895 or was color blind.

"Ladies, are you ready?" Cyril asked jovially as he descended the stairs behind me. "A beautiful day to get married, don't you agree?"

Every day in this part of the world seemed to be a beautiful day. As to whether or not it was a good one to get married, well, I had no answer for that. But he did look rather smashing in a black suit with a white rosebud boutonniere.

"Is it just the four of us?" Aunt Butty asked.

"A couple of friends will be joining us," Cyril assured us. "Wayne Palmer, you met him at the party. Trying to get him in my next film, you see. Good press and all. And an old friend of Lola's. Dolly something."

I and found it interesting Wayne Palmer was attending the wedding. He hadn't seemed particularly close to either Cyril or Lola, and I still wondered what he was doing hiding in the bushes. He'd seemed to be looking for someone all evening, had he found whoever it was?

The jangle of a telephone sounded from somewhere in the house. At the butler's beckoning, Cyril excused himself. He was gone only a short while, but on his return, he was beaming broadly.

"That was a friend of yours, Ophelia. Chaz? He's arrived safely at his friend's home here in California. I invited him to join us at the restaurant."

"Oh, that's brilliant, thank you," I said. "You'll love Chaz. He's good fun." Not to mention handsome, but I decided keeping mum was the better part of valor. After all, it might be that Lola didn't know her future husband's proclivities. Or it may be that I was wrong altogether. No sense rocking the boat.

Once Lola finally joined us—dressed in a simple white sheath dress with a little white hat perched on her platinum curls—she looped her arm through Cyril's. "Come on, honey. Let's get married!"

We climbed in the Bentley and Sam drove us into town. Lola chatted the whole way, clearly excited about her upcoming nuptials. A contrast to the sharp, calculating woman I'd previously witnessed. I was still struggling to determine who the real Lola was.

The newly opened Beverly Hills City Hall was a marvel. Cool, white stone stretched up into a clear, blue sky. On the very top of the cupola was a dome of blue mosaic topped with a gold crown. Wide steps—graced on either side with swaying palms—swept gently up to a magnificent arched entryway.

Inside Wayne Palmer was already waiting for us, looking a little nervous and uncomfortable. Like a man who'd been invited to a party where he didn't know or like anyone. Cyril shook his hand in a manly fashion and then nattered about the movie business and how perfect Palmer would be for his next picture. Palmer nodded politely but seemed otherwise uninterested.

Next to Wayne Palmer stood a young woman about Lola's age, but without the looks. Her features were pinched and mousy as if she were turning her nose up at the world. Equally mousy brown hair was done in a simple updo and topped by a plain straw cloche that was a few years out of date. Her simple day dress was an unfortunate lavender-gray which did her doughy complexion no favors.

For a moment I wondered if she was the woman I'd seen in the bushes, then realized she couldn't be. She was far too young. And the woman in the bushes hadn't been wearing glasses.

"Dolly, honey! You came!" Lola greeted her friend with genuine warmth.

"I would never have imagined Lola would be friends with such a plain looking woman," I said softly to Aunt Butty.

"Nor would I. But Cyril says they've been friends for a number of years. Since long before Lola made her debut on the silver screen. Quite poor, apparently. Dolly that is. Lola does what she can for her, but the unfortunate soul is determined to be miserable. Some people are like that."

This new information added layers of complexity I hadn't expected from the movie star. She'd mostly come across as completely self-obsessed, and yet here she was, caring for a friend she could have easily dumped by the wayside long ago.

A thirty-something woman in a smart, town tailored dress of teal silk strode up to us. "Brumble-Burns wedding party?" Her voice was smooth and cultured, her tone no-nonsense.

Cyril confirmed that we were the party, and she shook hands with both him and Lola. "Miss Helen Stern.

Secretary to Judge Arnott. Follow me, please." She turned and strode away, sensible heels clacking against marble.

She led us through the rotunda, down a short hall, to a small chapel-like room. A white-haired man in a black gown greeted us while Miss Stern got everyone to stand in their proper places. Then Judge Arnott droned on about the sanctity of marriage and so forth before launching into the vows.

As Cyril repeated his vows, I noticed Wayne Palmer fidgeting, tugging at his necktie as if it were strangling him. It was an odd reaction. Was he bored? Perhaps the thought of matrimony gave him a rash?

Perhaps he was the "he" Cyril and Carter were arguing about the night of the party. Surely not. Why would Cyril invite Palmer to his own wedding if he wanted his butler to stop seeing him? Perhaps Palmer's discomfort came not from being the subject of the argument, but from having realized overheard the argument and realized what it was about.

Now Lola was reciting her vows. I forced my attention back to the matter at hand.

"To love and to cherish, 'til death us do part," Lola repeated.

I couldn't have told you why, but at her words, a shiver went down my spine. As if someone had stepped on my grave.

Outside city hall, Wayne shook Cyril's hand, kissed Lola on the cheek, and congratulated both of them. "Sorry, but I must dash," he said apologetically. "Another engagement."

"Of course, of course," Cyril said. "Thank you for coming." As Wayne scurried off, Cyril turned to the rest of us. "Brunch at Cairo's is just the thing!"

My stomach certainly agreed with him. And I couldn't wait to see Chaz.

Cairo's turned out to be a lovely little spot not far from city hall. It was very low key on the outside, but the inside was stunningly beautiful. Lush, potted plants filled every corner while crystal chandeliers dripped from the high ceiling. The walls were painted in Ancient Egyptian-themed murals and the chairs and benches were upholstered in tan-and-salmon-striped damask.

Chaz was already there looking exceedingly handsome in a dark suit. He suitably impressed the ladies by bowing over their hands as he was introduced around. Lola fluttered her lashes at him, despite being a newly married woman. Her husband didn't appear to notice. He was too busy staring at Chaz himself.

We were seated in one of the more intimate booths, and immediately a black-and-white-garbed waiter brought a bucket of champagne to the table. We all cheered—except for Dolly—at the popping of the cork.

"It's too early to be drinking, don't you think?" Dolly said tartly, eyeing us all from behind her thick glasses.

"Oh, lighten up, Dolly," Lola chided. "It's my wedding day!"

To which we cheered again.

Aunt Butty raised her glass. "A toast to the happy couple. May you have a long and satisfying marriage."

"Hear! Hear!" Chaz agreed.

"I'll drink to that," Cyril agreed. And down the hatch went the champagne. "To my lovely bride!" Another glass disappeared, but the waiter immediately reappeared with a new bottle.

The brunch was delightful. In addition to some truly marvelous bubbly, we were served an extraordinary spread. Which was fortunate as I was half starving.

Plates appeared under our noses, piled with luscious servings of eggs benedict. I found it amusing when Cyril referred to the rounds of bread as "English muffins" since they were nothing like muffins in the least. Though I supposed they were quite similar to a crumpet, so perhaps something got lost in translation. In any case, the bread was piled with ham, topped with poached eggs, and half drowned in a gloriously rich, yellow Hollandaise sauce. Murder on the waistline. I utterly approved.

There were many more dishes: fresh berries in cream, buttery croissants with jam (delicious, but not nearly as good as one finds in France), sautéed veal and kidneys, potato cakes, and fish fillets, among other things. There was so much food, by the time we finished, it was a wonder I wasn't splitting my seams. It was astonishing to think that there was a Depression going on. You'd never know it based on this meal… or the Hollywood lifestyle in general.

Chaz and Cyril chatted about the business of making movies. I was surprised to find Chaz so knowledgeable. He'd never before expressed a particular interest in film.

"My friend, Archie, has been in the biz awhile," he explained to Cyril. "Just finished up a movie with Marlene Dietrich. Comes out this October. *Blonde* Venus, it's called. Too thrilling. He's been teaching me the ropes, so to speak."

"Are you interested in appearing on screen yourself?" Cyril asked, eyeing Chaz closely. "I could get you a screen test."

Chaz barked a laugh. "Me? You jest. I'm afraid I'm not nearly as handsome as Archie."

"I don't know who this Archie person is," Lola interrupted, fluttering her long, false lashes, "but he must be a dreamboat if he's handsomer than you."

To which Chaz blushed appropriately, although the man hadn't a shy bone in his body. "You are too kind, Mrs. Brumble."

She winced. "Call me Lola." Her tone was rife with meaning. Too bad for her she was barking up the wrong tree.

"Well, now, if you'll excuse us, I'm going to whisk my lovely wife away for some private time." Cyril beamed from ear to ear. As if he couldn't believe he was married to such a stunning creature. He seemed completely oblivious to her flirting.

Lola gave us a sunny smile. She seemed genuinely happy. Gone was the demanding, pouting bride-to-be and in her place was the stunning starlet of the silver screen. How astonishing.

"I'll be going, too," Dolly said in a strident voice that carried to nearby diners, causing a few to turn their heads. "I've had quite enough of the hoi polloi for one day."

"I don't think she knows how to use that term correctly," Chaz murmured as Dolly said her goodbyes to the newly married couple.

"Not in the slightest," I agreed.

Once Dolly had departed, we wished Cyril and Lola our best. Cyril assured us he'd send Sam back to take us home, but that we were to take our time and enjoy the rest of the champagne and food.

"Well, I never would have believed it if I hadn't seen it with my own eyes," Aunt Butty said as the two of them strolled arm-in-arm from the restaurant. She flagged down a waiter and ordered two mimosas.

"What's that, Aunt?"

"Cyril marrying a woman. And one half his age. I expected he'd remain a bachelor, if you know what I mean."

"Didn't you say he'd fallen in love with a woman before?" I asked. "What about that girl he took up on the roof for a picnic?"

"A picnic. Is that what they're calling it?" Chaz said slyly.

Aunt Butty ignored him. "That was *before*. I don't think he *realized* then. About men, I mean."

"Maybe he doesn't just like men," Chaz suggested. "Maybe he swings both ways. It happens, my friend—" he broke off as if realizing he was about to reveal a deep, dark secret that wasn't his to keep. "I know people," he finished lamely.

"Do you suppose it's real?" I mused. "Cyril and Lola's marriage?"

"Who can say? If it works for them, one can but wish them well." Aunt Butty shook her head and downed her mimosa.

"Something feels off, though, doesn't it?" I'd been getting that feeling since we first arrived.

"Definitely. But I'm sure it isn't any of our business."

"As if that ever stopped us," I said dryly.

"You honestly think there's something going on more than just an older man marrying a younger woman?" Chaz lifted a brow.

"I have a feeling..." I twisted my glass between my fingers. "I just can't quite put my finger on it." I turned to Chaz. "What did you think about the happy couple?" I wished he could have met Wayne Palmer. Now there was a character who set my senses tingling. And not in a good way.

"Cyril is an interesting man. Rather at odds with himself, I'd say. Not uncommon in his situation. Trying desperately to be something acceptable and failing miserably."

I gave him a sad look. "That's understandable."

"Unfortunately, it is," he agreed. "On the other hand, he clearly does dote on Lola, though perhaps not in an entirely sexual way. Almost…almost in a possessive way."

"Like she's a china doll and he wants to own her," I murmured.

"Something like that, yes," he agreed.

"Nonsense," Aunt Butty snapped. "I've known him for years. He's never been like that."

"Perhaps not," Chaz soothed, "but Hollywood changes people. Archie's told me enough stories that's become obvious."

"I really need to meet this Archie," I said.

Chaz smiled. "That can be arranged. Now, Lola…she's almost exactly what I'd expect from a Hollywood starlet: spoiled, selfish, obsessed with material possessions and attention. And yet she does seem to have a soft spot for Cyril."

"When she's getting her way," Aunt Butty said.

He gave her a nod. "Yes. That seems to be the case. This may simply be a marriage of convenience. Nothing more to it than that."

"You're probably right," I admitted. "But like I said, I've got a feeling…"

"You and your feelings." Aunt Butty flagged down the waiter. "I think we're going to need more mimosas."

Chapter 6

For the next couple of days, Aunt Butty and I were forced to knock about on our own while Cyril and Lola had a mini honeymoon. The chauffeur, Sam, kindly drove us around and showed us some of the sights while Carter, Cyril's man servant, kept us in cocktails, chocolate bonbons, and reading material by the pool.

On the first day, Sam drove us over to Greystone Manor. The mansion—for there was no other word to describe it—was massive. Perched high on a hill, pale gray stone stretched against impossibly blue sky while well-tended lawns stretched downward toward the road.

"It's what they call a Tudor revival," he explained as we wound through the hills. "Built it back in 1928."

"Practically new, then," Aunt Butty said, craning her neck to get a good look out the car window. "How could it be haunted?"

"Well, four months after Ned Doheny moved in with his wife and five children, he and his secretary, a man named Plunkett, were found dead in one of the spare rooms."

"Ghastly!" Aunt Butty sounded delighted. "Who murdered whom?"

Thrilled with having a captive audience, Sam continued. "Story has it, Plunkett was angry Doheny wouldn't give him a raise, so he shot Doheny then turned the gun on himself in despair. That's the official story, anyway."

"What's the unofficial story?" I asked, rolling down the window to better see the peaks and turrets. It was a lovely house. What seemed like hundreds of windows sparkled in the sun and imposing wrought iron gates blocked the way up the drive. I could well imagine an exclusive party on these grounds, the glittering Hollywood elite all in attendance.

"According to gossip, it was the other way around," Sam said. "It was Ned Doheny that killed his secretary then himself."

"What do you think happened?" Aunt Butty asked.

"Doheny wasn't buried with the rest of the family in the Catholic cemetery, so what does that tell you?" Sam eyeballed us in the rearview mirror, one golden eyebrow raised.

"That he committed suicide," I said. It was the one reason a Catholic couldn't be buried in a Catholic cemetery. It was the same for the Church of England where my father was a parish priest.

Sam nodded. "Got it in one."

Since the house wasn't open to the public, he drove us around so we could view the stunning grounds, reminiscent of the finest formal gardens of England with neat box hedges and perfectly trimmed rose bushes. But for all it's glory, there was a darkness to it, too. As if the deaths that had occurred there somehow tainted the place.

"It's a beautiful property," Aunt Butty mused. "They should shoot a film here, don't you think?"

"Lucy Doheny wouldn't have it," Sam said. "She owns it now and her word is law. But you're right. It would make a great setting."

"For a murder mystery," I muttered. I was betting that the Doheny/Plunkett murder suicide wouldn't be the last dark deed done at this manor.

On the second day, Chaz rang me up. "Archie's throwing a little soiree tonight," he said without preamble. "Nothing fancy. You should come. Wear a nice frock and bring Aunt Butty." He gave me the address and rang off without preamble.

The rest of the day was spent in a flurry of activity as Aunt Butty and I selected our gowns, had Maddie set our hair, and buffed and polished every inch of our bodies in preparation. Chaz had assured me it would be a "small gathering, just a few friends," but I knew Chaz's idea of a "small" gathering could easily mean over one hundred people.

Archie's bungalow was surprisingly modest, set in a quiet street not far from Cyril's studio. I'd expected a movie start to live somewhere more glamorous.

"He's just getting started," Aunt Butty assured me. "I'm sure he'll move up eventually, but he's probably one of those poor, starving artists right now."

What she knew about starving artists was beyond me, but I followed her up the walk to the charming little house. Every light in the place was on and music and laughter spilled from the open door.

We walked in to find the front room packed with glamorous people in sparkling gowns and dark tuxedos. I was glad I'd worn my Jean Patou. The evening dress had a Grecian flair and was elegant enough for any Hollywood party.

Chaz waved at us from the other side of the room before squeezing his way through the crowd. He swooped down to kiss our cheeks. "You came, delightful! Come darlings. You must meet Archie."

Somehow, we managed to squirm our way through to where a baby grand was set up. A dark-haired young man sat at the piano, long fingers dancing across the ivories. The tune was jaunty and fun, and his talent was obvious. When the tune finished, Chaz leaned over.

"Archie, come meet my dear friend, Lady Rample and her aunt, Lady Lucas."

The young man glanced up and I swear my mouth fell open. He could just about have been Chaz's twin! The same strong jaw. The same smoldering dark gaze. The same sardonic twist to the lips. And that little cleft in the chin.

"Ophelia, Butty, this is my good friend, Archie Leach."

"Please," Archie stood up and gave us a bow, "Call me Cary. It's my stage name, but I simply can't get Chaz to call me by it."

Chaz rolled his eyes. "Cary Grant? It's a ridiculous name. What's wrong with Archibald Leach?"

Archie—or rather, Cary—shook his head in amusement. "Thank you for coming, ladies. Would you like a drink?"

"Anything with whiskey," I said.

"Come on, Chaz, let's get these ladies some cocktails."

"Goodness me," Aunt Butty said as the two walked away. "They could be twins."

"It's astonishing," I agreed. "Do you suppose they were…you know? *Good* friends?"

Aunt Butty raised a brow. "I would think it would be rather like making love to oneself."

Before I could reply, I caught sight of another handsome man across the room. "Look, darling, it's Gary Cooper!"

Aunt Butty had to rise up on tiptoes to see over the crowd. "We must catch him, Ophelia! Hurry!" Without waiting for Chaz and Cary to return with our drinks, she plunged wildly into the crowd.

Fearing she might get trampled—or more likely trample someone else—I plunged in after her, squeezing my way between two starlets who were deciding whether or not to bleach their hair blonde or stay brunette. I jostled the elbow of a portly man and nearly sloshed his drink on him, to which I apologized profusely. And I rammed my own elbow into the ribs of another man who thought grabbing my posterior was amusing.

Gary Cooper was just a few feet ahead of us when he suddenly turned and made his way toward the front door.

Aunt Butty stopped, grabbed my arm, and shouted, "He's getting away!"

She charged through the crowd, dragging me after her, shoving people right and left. But alas, by the time we could get to the door, Gary Cooper had escaped through it and was striding purposefully down the pavement. He hopped into his car—the same one he'd been driving at the engagement party—and took off into the night.

"Oh, dear," I said. "There he goes."

Aunt Butty actually stamped her foot. "Curses! Foiled again. I swear, one of these days I will get that man."

I had no doubt she would. Poor Gary Cooper.

When Cyril and Lola returned Saturday evening, Lola asked if we wanted to join her on a shopping expedition, I was more than happy to do so. Aunt Butty needed no urging, either. Especially when Lola assured her we would lunch at one of the most popular Hollywood hotspots.

"Everyone eats there, dontcha know. Jean Harlow, Carole Lombard..."

"What about that divine Gary Cooper?" Aunt Butty demanded, clearly not over his most recent escape from her clutches.

"Oh, sure. All the time," Lola said airily.

"Done. Let me get my hat." Aunt Butty strode off for one of her monstrosities while I excused myself to touch up my face and grab my handbag.

Within minutes we were swooping down the drive, headed for Wilshire Boulevard and a department store called Bullock's Wilshire, which amused me no end. Lola assured us it was, "Quite upscale, honey." I could only take her word for it.

The building turned out to be a stunning, new art deco with a massive tower topped in copper. The moment Sam pulled up to the porte-cochere, a liveried valet dashed out to open our doors.

Inside stretched an elegant foyer of travertine tile and high ceilings with massive chandeliers. Lola led us straight to the vaulted Perfume Hall. My senses were immediately assaulted by every perfume known to mankind and then some. Both Aunt Butty and Lola made purchases, but I lingered around the edge of the hall, trying to avoid getting spritzed in the face by some overeager sales girl.

We took one of the brass, nickel, and gunmetal lifts upstairs to browse low glass cases filled with accessories and rosewood stands displaying designer clothing. Live mannequins stood or strolled about, showing off dresses and pantsuits and hats.

"We can check out the salons upstairs," Lola suggested. "That's where the real couture is."

"I'd much rather visit the tearoom," Aunt Butty said. "I'm feeling a bit peckish."

"Well, then, let's go!" Lola agreed.

We took the lifts to the top floor where the dessert-themed tearoom stood. The walls were papered in green silk, tables draped in cream linen, and chandeliers dripping with so many dazzling crystals, it was a wonder they didn't pull down the ceiling on our very heads.

We were seated immediately and served surprisingly well-brewed tea, finger sandwiches in a variety of flavors—beef and horseradish, cucumber and cream cheese, chicken salad—and a stunning array of desserts, from mini fruit tartlets and macarons to rich petite fours and caramel drenched blueberry pudding, each more delicious than the last. It was no wonder they were famed for their desserts.

"Mae West shops here," Lola confided as she nibbled on iced lemon cookies. "So does Marlene Dietrich. All the best people do, you know. It *pays* to be seen here."

As we enjoyed our repast, women in haute couture gowns strolled the aisles, twisting and turning and posing so patrons could get a good look. Apparently, one could order oneself a gown right there while one was having tea!

"Oh, that wrap is perfect," Lola squealed, pointing to a sheer number shot through with gold thread. "It's just like the one that went missing."

"You lost a wrap?" I asked.

"Not lost, honey," she tittered. "I couldn't lose something in my own house, could I? No, someone took it during the pool party. I'm sure of it."

"Why would anyone do that?" Aunt Butty asked. "Surely all the attendees were friends of yours."

Lola shrugged. "Who knows? Maybe they wanted to sell it or something. People do that, you know. Sell things that belong to famous people."

"And you're famous enough for that, are you?" Aunt Butty murmured. Fortunately, the music was loud enough Lola didn't hear her.

My mind immediately went to the woman in the bushes. Could she have simply been a common thief taking advantage of the distraction of a party to slip in and snag some expensive knickknacks? But why steal a wrap?

Lola caught the attention of a severe-looking woman in a black dress. They had a brief, whispered conversation and the woman walked away, leaving Lola with a satisfied expression. She eyeballed my plate. "Done. She'll have the new wrap delivered to the car. Now, are you going to eat all that cake?"

I fingered my knife. "Yes. Yes, I am."

After a long afternoon shopping, my feet ached. I was never so glad to climb into a car and head away from the city.

As we swooped up the drive, the house came into view. "What the Sam Hill?" Lola said.

I leaned forward to get a better view. A crowd of black Ford cruisers surrounded the house. Each had neat, white lettering on the side of the doors which I couldn't quite make out at this distance. But I did recognize the uniforms of the men milling about.

"What are the police doing here?" I wondered aloud.

"Probably a break in. Cyril was reading about it in the paper the other day. Lots of them going on. He was talking about getting more security." Lola seemed unperturbed; she was too busy admiring her purchases, particularly her new wrap.

"How exciting," Aunt Butty chortled.

I frowned, once again recalling the woman I'd seen hiding in the bushes during the party. She did seem to be looking for someone. Or something. Could she have broken in?

The chauffeur had to halt the car quite a distance from the house, thanks to the police vehicles. As he came 'round to let us all out, a man in a rumpled, dark-gray suit approached us. He was followed by a couple of uniformed officers, both ridiculously young and eager.

"Mrs. Brumble?" Gray Suit asked. He was a tall, thin man with a large Adam's apple and watery blue eyes. If he had any hair, it was completely covered by a brown fedora which clashed hideously with his suit.

"Miss Burns," Lola corrected. "I'm not changing my name. For *obvious* reasons. What the devil is going on here?"

"Detective Aarons, ma'am," Gray Suit said half-apologetically, touching the brim of his hat. "I'm afraid I have some bad news. Would you..." He glanced around with a frown. "Maybe you'd like to sit down somewhere?"

"I'm perfectly capable of standing," Lola snapped. "Now what is going on?"

Aarons cleared his throat. "I'm afraid that your husband has, well, passed on."

Lola stared at him with a hard expression. "What do you mean?"

"We got a call this morning, ma'am. From your man, Carter. Cyril Brumble is dead."

"Dead." She repeated it, her wide eyes blinking rapidly as if she couldn't quite take it in. "You must be mistaken. Cyril was in perfect health this morning."

"It wasn't his health, Miss Burns," Aarons said cautiously.

Lola stamped her foot. "Stop dithering, Detective."

"I'm sorry, ma'am, but I'm afraid your husband was murdered."

Chapter 7

After assuring us the police would be done soon, that he'd need to speak with us later, and to please stay out of the house for now, Aarons returned to the crime scene, leaving the uniformed officers with us. To guard us, perhaps. Or to eavesdrop. Either way, their presence certainly put a damper on things.

"Perhaps you ladies would like to sit in the summer house while the police finish up. I can get Carter to bring some refreshments," Sam suggested. He spoke to all of us, but his gaze was on Lola.

Lola blinked at him as if his words hadn't quite registered, but Aunt Butty patted his arm. "Wonderful idea, dear boy. You go arrange things. Where is this summer house?"

He pointed down a narrow path and then took off for the house at a lope. Aunt Butty put her arm around Lola's thin shoulders. "Come, my girl. Let's have a bit of a sit down, shall we? I think a spot of tea and a bit of a rest are just what we need to help us manage this shock, don't you think?"

The path wound down the hill, through thick, lush foliage until it came to an end in front of a small building that looked like a Swiss chalet, only much smaller. French doors opened onto a single room, just large enough for a settee, coffee table, and a couple of chairs. It was the perfect place for relaxing on a warm summer day.

Lola sank onto the settee while Aunt Butty and I took up residence in the chairs. The police officers stood guard outside without a word or glance. It was unfortunately easy to forget they were there. I kept having to remind myself that anything we discussed would likely be reported to the detective in charge.

"I'm so sorry, Lola," I said. "What a terrible thing. I understand what you're going through, so if you want to talk, I'm here for you." I did, indeed, know. While my Felix hadn't been murdered, he had died rather abruptly, leaving me a young widow without a clue. I had been in quite a bit of shock. At least for a while. I'd been inordinately fond of Felix, although not passionately in love. So while I'd been shaken, I hadn't been devastated. I had a feeling Lola was much the same. Hers and Cyril's had clearly not been a grand passion. How could it be?

Lola gave me a wan smile. A single tear slid dramatically down her cheek, and yet her eyes remained unreddened. In fact, she looked more angelic and serene than like a grieving widow. "You're very kind. I don't know how—"

The butler chose that moment to arrive. I noticed his eyes were red rimmed as if he'd been crying. I supposed that he'd worked for Cyril for some time and was probably fond of him. Well, more than fond, perhaps, based on what I'd overheard at the party. Also, he was no doubt worried about future employment. Would Lola keep him on now her husband was dead?

Carter placed the tray—loaded with tea, alcohol in an icy shaker, and piles of cheese and crackers, fresh fruit, and cookies—onto the low table in front of the settee. My stomach gave a rumble, but I had something more pressing on my mind.

"Carter," I said, "I don't suppose the police would let me in the house to use the necessary?"

He looked blank for a moment, then his expression cleared. "Ah, yes, my lady. I'm certain that can be arranged. If you will follow me?"

"Back in a tick," I assured Aunt Butty and Lola. But Aunt Butty was already elbow deep in the food and Lola was pouring herself a rather large cocktail from the shaker.

Carter murmured something to the police officers, then turned and wended his way down the path toward the house. I followed close behind. The police had better let me through or there would be a disaster! In the meantime, I figured I could do some—what was it those American detectives called it? —fishing.

"It's terrible what happened to Cyril," I said to Carter's back.

"Yes. It is," he said stoically without turning around. Though I was certain I saw his black clad shoulders tense just ever so slightly.

"Do you know what happened?" I stepped over an uneven paver, managing somehow not to trip in my high-wedged espadrilles.

"I'm afraid I found the master in his bedroom this morning. Once I had recovered from the shock, I called the police." His voice held absolutely no expression whatsoever. He could give any English butler a run for his money.

"Oh, dear. That's ghastly. How terrible for you." I meant it. Having seen a few dead bodies in my time, it was not something I relished. I couldn't imagine what it must be like for someone not used to it. Heavens, was I used to it? That was a terrifying thought.

"It was rather shocking," he admitted finally.

"What time did you, ah, find him?"

"Shortly after eleven. However, I believe he'd been dead for some time."

"Geez." I suddenly remembered Lola's rush to get us out of the house. How she'd been the one to instigate the shopping trip but had arrived flushed and distracted. Could she have offed her husband, then used the shopping trip, and Aunt Butty and myself, as an alibi? "I don't suppose you, ah, know how he died?"

"I'm afraid he shot himself."

I blinked. Shot himself? "As in suicide?"

"Yes, my lady. There was a note."

I rolled that around in my brain. Surely not. Cyril hadn't at all struck me as the sort to do such a thing. How ghastly for everyone concerned. I grabbed Carter's arm and spun him around to face me, suddenly forgetting the urging of my bladder.

"Tell me exactly what happened."

His expression was grim, and I half expected him to tell me to shove off, but he didn't. "He was meant to be at a meeting this afternoon, so I went to wake him. Instead, I found him dead on the floor with a wound to the head and a gun near his hand. I was quite stunned, you understand."

I nodded. "Of course, you were." I gave his arm a sympathetic squeeze before letting go.

"I checked to... to make sure he was... you know."

Dead. "Of course."

"No pulse. And he was quite cold and stiff."

Rigor mortis. I'd learned all about that after my previous experiences with dead bodies. It meant he'd been dead for probably at least six hours. Maybe more. Likely he'd died early in the morning when we'd all been home. But a gunshot would have woken me, surely. And I hadn't heard one.

"And the note?" I asked.

"On his dressing table."

"What did it say?"

He frowned. "It was very odd. Rambling. Didn't make much sense. In it he apologized to Miss Burns. Claimed this was the only way to right the wrong he'd done her."

"How bizarre."

"Indeed," he agreed. "It did seem most strange."

"And you're certain he wrote it?"

"It was in his own hand."

I frowned. If Lola had been in the room, surely, she would have noticed her husband offing himself. "Lola and Cyril didn't sleep in the same room?"

He cleared his throat. "She has her own bedroom. They have a unique arrangement."

I'll say. "Right. Well, lead on. Matters are pressing, I'm afraid."

The facts swirled around and around in my head. A wound to the head. A gun beside the body. A suicide note that made no sense. And a gunshot in the middle of the night that no one heard, even in a house full of guests.

As Alice would say: Curiouser and curiouser.

Carter managed to smooth things over with the detectives so I could use the cloakroom. Refreshed, I exited, intent on rejoining Lola and Aunt Butty. But as I passed through the living room, I was stopped by Detective Aarons.

"Mrs. Rample!" He strode across the room, his cheap, scuffed shoes thumping lightly against the carpet.

"That's *Lady* Rample," I said in my haughtiest tone. Long experience told me that the best way to deal with certain types of individuals—policemen being one of those—was to play lady of the manor to the hilt. It was the only way to avoid getting plowed under.

"Oh, sorry. *Lady* Rample then." He gave me a wry grin, which sat surprisingly well on his rugged face. It was not a handsome face. His nose was far too big and his lips far too thin, but it was a surprisingly nice face. Comforting. I'd just bet it helped a lot getting suspects to spill the goods. "I know it's been a shock, but I've got a few questions for you if you feel able. It would really help us."

I gave an inner smirk. If I felt able. Never let it be said that murder swayed me from my civic duty. Still, it wouldn't do to let on. Leave a few cards up the sleeve and all that. "If it's necessary. Fire away." I winced a little at my word choice. He didn't seem to notice, although if he was any sort of detective, I'd bet my last farthing he did.

He waved for me to sit and I took up residence in a comfortable arm chair. He perched on the edge of the couch. "Carter informs me that you're a guest here. All the way from England. Come for Mr. Brumble's wedding to Miss Burns."

"Yes. That's right."

"How do you know the deceased?" He pulled out a stubby pencil and a notebook and flipped it open.

"Well, I don't. Or rather, I didn't. Not before arriving. My aunt, Lady Lucas, knows him from her days in New York. He invited her, and she brought me along."

Aarons nodded. "And you've been here how long?"

"We arrived here in Hollywood five days ago."

"Carter also informed me that you left the house this morning at ten o'clock along with your aunt and Miss Burns."

"That's right."

He jotted something in his notebook. "Where did you go?"

"To a place called Bullock's Wilshire for some shopping. Then their tearoom for a late luncheon."

"And you returned to the house at three." It wasn't a question. He clearly knew exactly when we arrived.

"Yes. I'm surprised you're still here, actually."

He glanced up from his notebook, clearly startled. "Why do you say that?"

"Well, Carter told me he found the body at eleven, and if he called the police straight away—"

"Eleven?"

I was surprised by his surprise. "That's what he told me."

He tugged on his lower lip and muttered, "But the call didn't come through until almost o—" He broke off as if remembering he was speaking to a civilian. "Go on."

He was obviously going to say one. Why would Carter have waited so long. He did say he was in shock… I shook off the thought, determined to return to it later. "We arrived back, what, four hours later? And you're still here. Seems a long time for a suicide."

He frowned, a glimmer of suspicion lighting his eyes. "And why do you think it was a suicide?"

"I heard about the note." I didn't mention it was Carter who told me. I didn't want to get him into trouble with the authorities. Beside which, it's always a good idea to play things close to the vest, as they say.

"Ah." He eyed me closely. "Who told you?"

I gave him a bland smile. "Oh, you know. A little bird."

"The butler, no doubt. Something tells me you don't buy it."

I gave him a small smile. "Astute."

"Why's that?"

"Well, for one, Cyril wasn't the sort to... how do you say?... off himself. I'm quite certain if you speak to my aunt, she'll agree. And she's known him ever such a long time. Secondly, he'd just got married. And he commits suicide two days later? Seems a dashed odd time to do it. Then there was the note. According to Carter it made no sense. Rambling and so forth. Not the usual thing, is it? And then there's the woman in the bushes."

Aarons blinked. "The woman in the bushes?"

"Yes. During the engagement party. The one with Gary Cooper."

He blinked again. "Gary Cooper."

"Mm. Yes, you see my aunt is quite the fan."

"Of Cooper?"

"Indeed. Thinks he's marvelous." I didn't mention my own feelings about the movie star. I didn't want him to think I was simply another star-struck, approaching-middle-age woman. "She wanted to meet him, but alas! He left the party before we could make an introduction. So she ran after him." Aunt Butty would kill me for telling on her.

"Your aunt ran after Gary Cooper." He appeared amused.

"Yes. Well, only because she wanted to say hello. As you do. And maybe get an autograph, you know."

"Right."

"I followed along to make sure she didn't twist an ankle. The steps are rather uneven, don't you think?"

He coughed. "Er, yes. Very."

"But when we got to the top, he was already getting into his car."

"Such a shame."

"Oh, my aunt was *very* disappointed." I hoped I wasn't laying it on too thick.

He touched his lips with his fingertips as if holding back a smirk. "I'm sure."

"In any case, I turned to go back to the party and there she was."

"There who was?"

"The woman in the bushes, of course. She was hiding out and just sort of staring down at the party as if she was spying on someone. Then she saw me and ran away."

"Did you, ah, get a good look at her?"

"Of course. She was wearing this terribly ill-fitting suit. Cheap. Navy blue. Her hair was brown with a bit of gray in it. Not a lot. Just a few strands. Rather pretty, but very wan looking."

He scribbled in his notebook. "That's it?"

"That's it." I should probably have brought up the fact that Cyril and Carter had an argument that night. That Cyril was on the verge of firing Carter. Or even that Palmer was nearby during their argument and had likely overheard it all. Somehow, I just couldn't do it. I very much doubted Wayne Palmer was involved in Cyril's death, and Carter seemed to care too much for Cyril to harm him. Beside which, regardless of what I thought, Aarons was convinced it was a suicide. No sense muddying the waters until I had something concrete to go on.

"And you think this could be related to Mr. Brumble's death?"

"That's not for me to say," I said tartly. "You're the policeman."

"Yes, I am."

"Now, if you'll excuse me. I need to rejoin my aunt. I'm sure she's overwrought." As if Aunt Butty was ever overwrought by anything. She was more likely the one to be causing someone to be overwrought.

"The aunt that chased Gary Cooper." Was that sarcasm in his tone?

"She didn't *chase* him. She merely followed him. With a great deal of eagerness." And with a huff, I stood and strode from the room. I could have sworn I heard Aarons stifling a laugh.

Chapter 8

"I'm telling you, it's utter poppycock," Aunt Butty insisted. "There is no way Cyril killed himself. I refuse to believe it."

It was after supper that night. Lola had excused herself and gone to bed, leaving us to our own devices. We'd meandered out to the pool where Carter had brought us nightcaps. Naturally, Cyril's death was on our minds. It was quite a shock. More so for Aunt Butty than for me since she'd actually known the man. Still, it felt very surreal and I was having a difficult time coming to grips with the fact that the lively little man whose wedding I'd just attended was now dead.

"You're certain?" I asked. "Could he have been depressed or... you know how hard it is to be…different." Preferring the company of men was not an easy life, seeing as how it was still illegal. At least in England. I'd no idea about America.

"Don't be daft. Cyril wasn't bothered by such nonsense. He was a powerful man here in Hollywood. No one would have turned him in."

"So why ever would he marry Lola?"

She shrugged. "He cared about her. Probably felt marrying her was a good way to protect himself from wagging tongues, just in case. Plus he probably felt protective of her, being alone in the world as she is and in need of guidance for her career. But it's not like he was forced into this. He told me himself they enjoyed each other's company. Most of the time, anyway. And no doubt both of them planned to take lovers on the side. He'd have no reason to be depressed about it. Besides, the man wasn't prone to melancholy."

"Alright, so I'm inclined to agree with you about it not being suicide. It's just... something is fishy."

She turned gimlet eyes on me. "What do you know, Ophelia?" Her tone assured me prevarication would not be tolerated.

"Right, so Carter told me he found the body around eleven this morning, but the police were still here at three. Why would they be here that long if it was a suicide?"

"I doubt they would," Aunt Butty agreed.

"So I mentioned that to Detective Aarons and he seemed surprised to hear that Carter found the body so early. He started to tell me what time the police were called, but then he stopped as if he remembered who he was talking to."

"Too smart for his own good," Aunt Butty said dryly.

"Rather. In any case, I'm certain he had started to say the time. One o'clock."

Aunt Butty sat up straighter. "Two hours after Carter found the body."

"Exactly. Why would he wait so long? He did say he was in shock, and that he called them once he'd calmed down, but that's still a long time. What happened in those two hours? Because something did, and it wasn't anything good."

Aunt Butty frowned. "What do you think happened?"

"I'm not sure," I admitted. "But this is what I think. Carter told me Cyril had been shot in the head, and the gun was near his hand. But based on rigor mortis at eleven this morning, Cyril had already been dead for several hours. Which means he would have had to shoot himself in the middle of the night."

"I'd have heard the shot," Aunt Butty insisted. "I'm not a heavy sleeper, as you know."

"I'd have heard it, too," I agreed. "There are only two ways I know for a shot to have occurred without us hearing it. The first is some other loud noise, which we know there wasn't or that would have awoken us."

"And the other?"

"A silencer."

Aunt Butty frowned. "That seems a dashed odd thing to put on a gun if one is going to shoot oneself."

"Exactly. And Carter didn't mention seeing one, so I'm betting there wasn't. I'll have to ask him to make sure."

She nodded. "Yes. Good plan. So if there wasn't a silencer..."

"If there wasn't a silencer, then he couldn't have shot himself. Someone else had to have done it and then left the gun on the scene in order to make it look like suicide."

"It makes more sense than Cyril offing himself."

"But why would someone want to murder him?" I asked, remembering the argument between Cyril and Carter. But Cyril hadn't fired the butler after all, therefore Carter had no reason to murder his boss.

"Who knows? These Hollywood types are volatile. Maybe someone didn't like his choice of star for his latest picture."

I sighed. "Right. So we've got a missing gunshot, a two-hour gap, and a note that doesn't make sense, at least according to Carter. Plus there's Lola insisting on going shopping with us at the last minute."

"You think she had something to do with it?" Aunt Butty's eyes were wide.

"There was certainly enough time for her to shoot him, then join us for shopping to give herself an alibi. She probably doesn't know about rigor mortis like I do."

"Then how does Carter know about it?"

Now that was a sticker. "Another thing I'll have to ask him."

She pursed her lips. "If it weren't for the fact she's in New York, I'd think it was Dorothea."

"Who the deuce is Dorothea?"

"Cyril's ex-wife."

I sat bolt upright, nearly sloshing my Vieaux Carré all over myself. "You never mentioned Cyril had an ex-wife!"

"Well it simply didn't cross my mind. It was such a long time ago really, and he hadn't seen her in a number of years. She's... well, she's been unwell, so she hasn't been out and about, if you know what I mean."

"No, Aunt, I do *not* know what you mean. I think you'd better explain."

"As you know, I met Cyril about twenty years ago. Give or take." Which would have put Aunt Butty in her late thirties or early forties, and Cyril in his mid-twenties. "I lived in New York for a time after Husband One bit the dust." Husband One being Henry Thorton the Third. Richer than Croesus and a bit of a dullard, if I recall. He'd keeled over from a heart attack after eating an entire pork pie.

"Right. Go on," I prodded.

"We were both heavily involved in theater. Cyril was interested in writing and directing, and I trod the boards, as they say."

That got me. "You were an *actress?*"

"Don't sound so astonished. I was rather good."

"You've certainly got the theatrics for it," I muttered.

"What's that dear?"

"Nothing. So you met Cyril on Broadway?"

"More like Broadway adjacent, but yes. In any case, I met his wife there, too. Dorothea Caron. Lovely girl. French. He married her after he broke it off with the other one…the one from the rooftop. We all used to get together at their apartment in Manhattan, run lines, drink wine, you know the sort of thing. They met there in New York. She was from France, he from Germany. There was, of course, the whole preferring other men thing, but I don't think Cyril realized it at the time, though the rest of us did. Still, they seemed a delightful couple."

"But?"

Aunty Butty shifted uncomfortably. "Dorothea was what one might call high-strung. Dreadful mood swings. Bright and cheerful one moment, darkly melancholy the next. Poor thing. And Cyril was distraught over it. Eventually she ended up in a sanitorium. It simply wasn't safe for her to be on her own, you see. It got to the point, well... Cyril had an opportunity out in Hollywood, so he took it."

"And left Dorothea locked up back in New York?"

"Couldn't be helped, I'm afraid. And the work out here allowed him to support her. Ensure she had the best care."

"But they did divorce."

Aunt Butty frowned. "Now there's the thing. They were only ever common law according to the state of New York. Legal enough there, but not out here. So there was no divorce, per se—they simply parted ways. Though Cyril would visit her when he was in New York."

"At the sanitorium?"

"Oh, no, she's out now. Has been for years. All cured, according to Cyril, though I doubt that. That sort of thing doesn't really get cured, does it."

"So she could have come out here and killed him," I mused.

"Doubtful. Why would she? He's been supporting her for years. Very generously, too. Without him, she'd be in the poor house."

"What does she look like?"

"Dark hair and eyes. Slender. About my height. Why?"

I told her about the woman in the bushes. "Sounds very like the woman you describe. But older."

"If it were Dorothea, surely she'd have joined the party. As I said, she and Cyril may no longer be together, but they are on friendly terms."

"But are she and Lola?"

My aunt's eyes widened. "Fair point. I've no idea."

"Exactly. And *that's* something I need to ask Lola." Because I couldn't imagine Lola sharing the spotlight with another wife.

"You think Dorothea could be a viable suspect?"

"Possibly," I said. "If she was the woman I saw. But I'd say Lola could be one, as well. After all, jealousy is a powerful motive for murder."

When I came down to breakfast the next morning, there was toast, jam, and coffee laid out in the dining room, but there was no one to be seen. I slathered a slice of toast with strawberry preserves, filled a cup with coffee dosed liberally with cream and sugar, and sauntered outside to enjoy my breakfast by the pool. I'd just polished off my toast when the chauffeur came around the corner of the house. He started when he saw me.

"Ah, Lady Rample. Sorry to disturb you. I was looking for Carter."

"Haven't seen him, I'm afraid. In fact, no one seems about."

"Well, I drove Miss Burns to the studio early this morning," Sam said by way of explanation.

I stared at him over the rim of my cup. I could hardly believe what I was hearing. I admit that while I'd been sad over the loss of Felix, I hadn't been devastated. But still, I'd had a decent mourning period. "She went to work?"

"Yes, ma'am," he drawled. "Kinda strange, if you ask me. Her husband just dyin' and all."

I set down my cup. "Very strange, indeed. How did she seem?"

He rubbed his jaw. "Determined." His tone was one of admiration. "Like she was gonna grab the bull by the horns, if you get my meanin'."

I did. "She's either very brave or... Well. People handle grief differently, don't they?"

"S'pose so, ma'am." He scratched his chin which looked like t could use a shave. "I do feel sorry for her."

"Of course you do. Any decent person would. By the by, the police say Mr. Brumble was killed very early Sunday morning. Did you happen to hear a gunshot sometime before dawn?"

"No, ma'am. But then my place is down the hill a way over the garage, and I sleep like a log. Probably wouldn't have heard anything." He gave me an assessing look. "Will tell you one thing, though."

I leaned forward, eager to hear what promised to be a juicy bit of gossip. "What's that?"

"Saturday night it was kinda late, and I got a bit hungry. So I went into the kitchen to sneak somethin' from the larder, and I heard voices. Loud. Real loud."

"Like an argument?" This *was* juicy.

"Yes, ma'am."

"Could you tell who it was?" Perhaps it had been Cyril's killer.

"Well, it was definitely Mr. Brumble. And he was fightin' with some woman. They was just screamin' and yellin' and carryin' on. So I grabbed somethin' and lit out quick. I was halfway back to my place when the woman came runnin' out of the house, jumped in a car, and drove away."

"Lola drove away?"

"No, ma'am. Weren't Lola. The woman I saw Mr. Brumble arguing with was a dark-haired woman. Older lady. Navy skirt and jacket. Looked real scared."

The woman from the bushes. Had to be. "What time was this?"

"Just past midnight, I think."

Which meant this woman, whoever she was, had probably been the last person to see Cyril Brumble alive!

Chapter 9

With breakfast out of the way, Lola out of the house, and Aunt Butty still abed, I decided it was time to track down the butler—Cyril's "man," as he'd referred to him. At this point, he was the most logical person to question as he'd discovered the body. I found him at the dining room table, polishing the silver, looking morose.

"Hello, Carter," I said, taking a seat across from him and propping my elbows on the table in an unladylike fashion.

He hesitated, one hand clutching a rag and the other a silver gravy boat. "Madam?" He looked a bit nonplussed.

"I'm surprised to see you hard at work this morning."

He blinked. "What else was I to do?"

"Well your employer just died, and you found him, so I half expected you to be out of commission. It would be entirely understandable."

He firmed his jaw. "Never. The work doesn't stop simply because... because Mr. Brumble has gone to be with his maker."

That was a delicate way of putting it. "Very true. I suppose Lola was of the same opinion. I heard she went off to the studio this morning."

This time his jaw took on a hard set as if he was trying to bite back some rather nasty words. "She has, perhaps, another agenda."

"Oh?"

He ducked his head and went back to polishing with more vigor than necessary. "It's not my place to say."

"Really?" I said archly. "You were awfully chatty before."

He sniffed. "That was before *she* was paying my salary."

"I see." So, Lola had told him to keep his mouth shut about her business now that she was in charge. Interesting.

Pushing him at the moment likely wouldn't do any good, so I got to the meat of the matter. "The police told me that Cyril died very early Sunday morning. Hours before you, ah, found him. But... well, I didn't hear the shot."

"You were no doubt sleeping."

"True. But my room is just across the hall from his, and I'm not a particularly heavy sleeper. I would have definitely heard a gunshot at three in the morning." Actually, I tended to sleep like the dead, but I most definitely *would* have heard a shot.

He mulled that over. "Likely that's true."

"Did you hear one?"

"Alas, no. My room is off the butler's pantry through the kitchen. Quite a way from Mr. Brumble. I wouldn't have heard a thing."

Right. "You said there was a gun near him when you found him."

"That's so. Lying just next to his hand as if it fell after he... well, you know."

"What kind of gun was it?"

He stared up at me with a blank expression. "No idea. I'm not particularly familiar with guns. I'm sure the police would know. But I can say it wasn't a particularly large one. Quite small, in fact."

Likely a small caliber, then. Which would mean the shot would have been more like a cork popping. "Do you know what a silencer is?"

He looked offended. "Of course. I've seen films."

"Did you notice one on the gun? Or anywhere in the room?"

He frowned. "No. Is it important?"

"Might be." I sighed. "You also told me rigor mortis had set in by the time you found him. That's how you knew he'd been dead awhile. I'm surprised you'd know about such things."

"I served in the Great War," he informed me haughtily. "I learned many things I wish I didn't know."

"Then how do you not know about guns?" I demanded.

"I was a conscientious objector. Raised Quaker. I couldn't shoot, but I wanted to do my part. So I was with the ambulance corps."

"The American Volunteer Motor Ambulance Corps?" I asked, impressed.

He nodded. "The same."

"You people did important work. I was a nurse."

"So you did, too."

We were silent a moment, lost perhaps in our own memories. Finally, I asked, "Is that why you didn't ring the police right away?"

He gave me a blank look. "What do you mean?"

"You told me you found Cyril at eleven, but Detective Aarons said the police weren't called until after one in the afternoon." Slight lie. Detective Aarons had started to tell me something but hadn't finished. Still, Carter didn't need to know that. "Is it because you knew he'd been dead awhile? That he'd killed himself?"

"Yes. Ah, yes. I was hoping Miss Burns would come back so she could contact them. Being the widow and all. But when she was still gone after several hours, I decided to call myself. I shouldn't have waited, I know. But I was in shock. Not thinking straight. I told the detective that, too, after he asked." He gave me a pointed look. Clearly Aarons had questioned him after I spilled the beans.

Carter's explanation seemed plausible, I suppose, but somehow, I didn't believe him. Not entirely. Something else had happened in those two hours between Carter finding the body and calling the police. I just had to figure out what.

The rest of the day I felt rather at loose ends. I wanted to question Lola, but she hadn't returned from the studio. Aunt Butty stayed in bed, claiming a headache. Based on the fact that she'd just lost an old friend, a bottle of very good scotch was missing from the liquor cabinet, and I knew she'd picked up three new books during our shopping trip, it was more likely she was using that as an excuse to stay in bed all day. As for the chauffeur and the butler, they'd given me all they could—or would—for the moment.

There was the cleaning woman, but she hadn't been to the house either Sunday or Saturday, and according to Carter, Lola had ordered him to tell the woman not to come today. So I wouldn't be able to talk to her until tomorrow at the latest. Mrs. Mendez, the woman who came to cook, had also been out from noon Saturday until this morning. And by the time I'd gotten up, she'd already been gone, having put together a few bits and pieces so Carter could make up meals the rest of the week. Which meant she was out for questioning.

Detective Aarons had ordered Aunt Butty and me to stay close. Though he'd not quite gone so far as to order us not to leave town. He'd claimed he might have further questions, but I wasn't holding my breath. He'd seemed pretty convinced it was murder. Which struck me as dashed odd based on the evidence at hand. Or rather, the strangeness of the evidence pointing to suicide.

I could go through Cyril's study. Men kept things in their studies they didn't want wives finding out about. Maybe he had a diary. A calendar. Something.

Fortunately for me, Cyril left his office door unlocked. The room was dim, curtains drawn against the afternoon sun. It was warm and a little musty, but I snapped on the light and strode to the desk.

There was one long drawer, very shallow. It had no lock, so I pulled it open, and it slid out surprisingly easily. Inside, neatly arranged in precise little rows, were pencils, pens, a bowl of paperclips, and other accoutrements one would expect. In addition, there was a black leather-covered notebook with the year stamped on the front: 1932. I took it out and laid it on the desk, sliding the drawer shut.

Carefully opening the cover, I realized that this was not a notebook or journal. This was a weekly planner of sorts. Each page had a date along the top and hours marching in a column down the left-hand side. Here and there in loopy blue ink were notations for various appointments.

I flipped to the date Aunt Butty and I had arrived. Sure enough, along the top of the page was the notation, "Butty and Lady R arrive."

A notation for the following evening was simply "party." And on the day of his wedding to Lola was the notation "city hall."

"Now that's interesting," I murmured. I would have assumed he would write something like "wedding" or "marriage." Perhaps some exclamation points. But "city hall?" It seemed so cold and impersonal. Then again, both Aunt Butty and myself had been suspicious of this marriage from day one.

I quickly flipped forward to Saturday, the day before Cyril died. The entire day was blank, no notations. No appointments. Not so much as a stray ink mark.

Frustration seethed inside me. Then again, what had I expected? That he'd leave the name of his killer neatly printed out across the page? I supposed I'd hoped that at the very least there might be an appointment. Or a notation that someone was in town. Like Dorothea.

I turned the page to Sunday. Again, a blank page. No doubt the police would declare that this meant he planned to commit suicide. That since there were no appointments on those days that he knew he wouldn't be around to keep them. I wasn't so sure.

I continued paging through the calendar. Over the next few days there were no appointments but once I got to later in the month, I found that the appointments resumed. Under September 15, 10 a.m. there was the notation: "Bob at Chasson's."

I had no idea who Bob was or what Chasson's was, but clearly that meant that he planned to attend this meeting. Why else would he write it in his calendar?

There were several other appointments and reminders throughout the calendar. Birthdays, parties, business meetings, and so forth. Everything you'd expect to see in the calendar of a busy and important individual. There was no indication to my mind that this was a man who planned to end his life. I supposed he could have decided his future plans were less important than ending it all, but I just didn't buy it.

I slipped the notebook back in its drawer and sat for a moment deliberating. This study was a small one. The desk sat facing the door. Behind me was a narrow window with the curtains pulled over it. To my right a cozy-looking armchair. To my left, against the wall, a narrow bookshelf with a few books.

I got up, wandered over to the bookshelf, and carefully inspected the spines. Not much to go on there. Mostly it was classic fiction. A few memoirs of famous men. A couple of history books. I took a few out and flipped through the pages hoping that perhaps a letter or something would magically fall out. But nothing did.

Along the bottom of the bookshelf were some file boxes each neatly marked with a year. I took out the one for 1932. Inside were a few contracts, some bank statements, that sort of thing. I didn't know much about the business of making movies, but it did seem that Cyril was running a little low on cash. In fact, if what I was reading was correct, he was flat broke. So how on earth could he afford to live in this house? Never mind throw pool parties. He must have been spending Lola's money.

I kept digging until I found a sheet of paper. Sure enough, it was a typed agreement—an IOU—signed by Cyril. It seemed he had borrowed a significant amount from Lola. Interesting.

At the very bottom of the box, I found a life insurance policy for the sum of one million dollars. Seemed a hefty amount, but Cyril was a movie director. He had a lot of influence in Hollywood, or so it seemed. And until I'd seen his bank statements, I would've thought he was worth a pretty penny. I quickly scanned the document and realized that the sole beneficiary was Lola. Again, very interesting. Granted she was his wife, but the policy had been taken out several months ago. Around the time he'd borrowed money from her. Perhaps it was to insure she'd get her money back if he died. Except, if he really did commit suicide, she'd never see a dime. If he was murdered, she'd want it to *look* like murder. She wouldn't fake a suicide.

Stuffing the documents back in the box, I tucked it away in its spot on the shelf. With nowhere left to search, I decided to make use of the telephone.

I picked up the receiver and gave quick instructions to the operator. Within a few moments, I was connected to the Villa de la Bella Mer.

"Mr. Singh," I said when he came on the line. "Were you able to get the message through as I asked you?"

"But of course, Lady Rample," he assured me. "I delivered the message promptly as instructed."

"And?" Why was my stomach in knots? Why was I so ridiculously nervous? It wasn't like I was sixteen and Hale was a new love. We were just… Well, I didn't know what we were just. But it wasn't anything that I should be nervous over. I prided myself on never being nervous when it came to men.

"Mr. Davis gave me a message to return to you."

The knots got tighter. "Yes?"

"He asked me to tell you that he was disappointed that you would be kept away longer than planned," Mr. Singh said in a slightly stilted voice as if he were reading from a cue card. "And he said that if you would like to speak to him, he could be available tomorrow evening via the telephone here."

Tomorrow evening. Which would make it morning for me. "Mr. Singh, please tell Mr. Davis that that would be most amenable."

"I will do so straightaway, Lady Rample," Mr. Singh assured me.

After hanging up with my aunt's butler, I found myself still assaulted by nerves to the point I was a bit queasy. There was but one thing for it. I left Cyril's study and headed straight for the drinks cart and a Vieux Carré.

Chapter 10

That night, Lola finally put in an appearance around nine. Aunt Butty and I had already dined on a simple meal of cold sliced meats, cheeses, and bread prepared by Carter and were enjoying cocktails around the pool. I heard a car drive up, a door slam, and then high heels clip-clopping on the wood floor followed by thumping on the stairs. About thirty minutes later, Lola clattered out on silver heels and wearing a snug, silver gown. Her white and silver wrap had a ruff of fur around the collar. She looked magnificent and not at all like someone who'd just lost her husband.

"Oh, *there* you are. I figured you'd have scatted off to England by now." She seemed a little tipsy already and took an odd little side-step as if slightly off balance.

"I'm afraid we'll have to rely on your hospitality a bit longer," Aunt Butty said. "The police have ordered us to remain here."

Actually, they'd ordered us to remain in the area, not here specifically, but I wasn't going to argue. Staying on the premises would allow me to continue my investigations into Cyril's death.

"Oh." Lola gave a little pout. One clearly well-practiced and which accentuated the voluptuous curves of her scarlet-painted lips. I'd seen it on the silver screen more than once. "I suppose that'll have to do. Well, I'm headed out. Party at the Ritz, doncha know. Simply everyone will be there, honey."

"But your husband just died," I said. "Shouldn't you be—I don't know—in mourning?" Wearing black at the very least.

She waved a hand. "Pish posh. That's so conventional. Who cares about convention?"

"The police, for one," Aunt Butty said tartly.

"The studio'll take care of them." Lola arched a brow. "Ain't got nothin' to worry about, honey. They'll fix it."

"You mean they'll happily cover up a murder?" I suggested.

"It wasn't a murder!" She stamped her foot, silver flashing in moonlight. "That idiot killed himself and messed up all my plans." She seemed to realize she'd given herself away and quickly added, "*Our* plans. We had a great future ahead of us. Cyril always said so."

"I don't believe it was suicide, Lola," I said gently. "Neither does Aunt Butty."

"Had to be. There was a note."

"I haven't seen a note, have you Ophelia?" Aunt Butty asked over the rim of her glass.

"No, I haven't."

"There you are. Neither of us have seen it. Have you, Lola?" Aunt Butty eyed her narrowly.

"Well... no," she admitted, sounding somewhat surprised. "But surely the police wouldn't lie about that."

"Of course not," I assured her, not entirely sure that was true. After all, a force that could be bought by a movie studio wasn't one to be trusted. Though Aarons had seemed an honest man. "But until either you or Aunt Butty can confirm it is in Cyril's handwriting, then..." I shrugged.

"Beside which, aren't you curious about what's in the letter?"

"Well, now you mention it," Lola admitted, propping her right fist on her hip. "I guess I am."

"There you go, then." Aunt Butty slapped the arm of her chair. "We need to get that letter from the police."

"I don't think they're going to fork it over just because we ask politely," I muttered.

"True, but Lola is his widow, and as such she has a right to see the note. And we, as her caring friends, will be there to help her along." Aunt Butty gave me a knowing look.

"Oh, would you?" Lola gushed, clasping her hands and fluttering ridiculously long eyelashes. "That'd be so nice of you."

"Of course. Anything for you, dear Lola," I said with my own fake flutter. Although my lashes weren't nearly as impressive.

"I'll ring the detective tomorrow," she assured us. "But for now, I'm off. Toodles." She gave us a finger wave and toddled off up the steps to the drive. Once again, I heard the slam of a car door followed by the roar of an engine quickly fading.

"Well, how do you like that?" Aunt Butty muttered.

"It's an odd way to react to someone's death. Especially someone you just married," I agreed.

"Do you suppose she's behind it? Or is she simply that callous?"

"Hard to say." I shook my head and got up to refill my cocktail. I told her about the million-dollar life insurance. "I can't see her killing him and covering up as a suicide. Not with that amount of money involved. It could simply be that the marriage was far more business arrangement than we realized, and she's simply getting on with things. We should definitely keep an eye on her. But at least we'll be able to see the note now. Find out exactly what it says. And whether or not Cyril actually wrote it, or if the killer left it behind to throw us off the scent."

The next day dawned bright and sunny. As if it did anything else here. Every day, it seemed, was much like the next. Did it never rain? I could simply kill for a lovely, cloudy day and a bit of drizzle.

"Good morning m'lady," Maddie said cheerfully as she marched into my room and flung open the curtains. A shaft of light spilled over my face, and I let out a groan. She was much too fond of early morning

"That Miss Burns already been up, dressed, and out of the house ages ago," Maddie informed me as she turned to the tray she'd placed on the table under the window. The clink of silver against porcelain rang in my ears.

"That's no good," I said, making a half-hearted attempt to sit up. "She promised me she was going to ring the detective."

"Oh, that she did," Maddie assured me. "First thing. She said to tell you that Detective Aarons bloke will meet you at the police station this afternoon. She left a note." She handed over a rumpled folded piece of paper.

I unfolded it and squinted at it. Sure enough, in barely legible handwriting, there was an address and a time. One o'clock.

"What time is it?" I asked.

Maddie handed me a steaming cup. "Just gone ten, m'lady."

I sniffed at the contents of the mug. "Coffee again?"

"No decent tea to be had 'round here, and that's a fact. Coffee will have to do."

I sighed. "Very well." I took a sip. Decent stuff, and liberally dosed with cream and sugar. "I think I'll wear the linen shift with the buttons today."

"Very well." Maddie turned and disappeared into the closet—Americans had them built in! No wardrobes, just lovely deep closets for storing loads of clothing.

I finished up my coffee, poured myself another cup, and then went about the business of repairing my hair and face. Half an hour later—suitably powdered and lipsticked—I headed down to breakfast.

The dining room was empty. No doubt Aunt Butty was still in bed. This would be an excellent time to make a few phone calls. Maybe Chaz would be free for a bit of shopping. But my stomach gave an unholy growl. Food first.

The sideboard was laden with chafing dishes of scrambled eggs, American style crispy bacon, and a rack of toast. It seemed Mrs. Mendez was back at her post. I made myself a bacon and egg sandwich and carried it with me to Cyril's study.

Closing the door gently behind me, I sat behind the desk, picked up the receiver, and gave the operator Archie's phone number.

"Hullo."

"Chaz, darling! It's Ophelia. What are you doing answering Archie's telephone?"

"He's out at the moment. Some meeting or other. What's up, love?"

"Something dreadful happened," I told him about Cyril's death. "The police think it's suicide, but I think it might be murder."

I sighed. "Trust you to find a dead body everywhere you go."

"I didn't actually find it this time, thank goodness. The butler did."

"Classic," Chaz said. "I am sorry, though. Cyril seemed a nice chap. Butty must be devastated."

"She's locked herself in her room for the day. Which leads me to the reason I called. I'm meeting Lola later today but am at loose ends at the moment. Wondered if you'd like to, I don't know, go shopping or drinks or whatnot."

There was a pause. "I'm afraid I can't. Not today."

It was unusual that Chaz wouldn't be available, particularly when drinks were involved. "What are you up to?"

"Archie got me a screen test," he said in a giddy rush. "It's this afternoon.

"Oh, my! Tell me *everything.*"

He quickly told me about Archie's latest film in which he wanted Chaz to play his brother. "People around here think we look alike. Which we don't, of course, but if it gets me a job in film, who cares."

I didn't bother pointing out that Archie/Cary and Chaz did indeed look very much alike. "I didn't know you were interested in becoming a film star."

"Well, I wasn't. Not until Archie suggested the screen test. I think it'll be good fun. And if it leads to a career, why not? My father's generosity isn't endless, you know." Chaz came from a very wealthy family and was given a monthly allowance, but there was always the worry it would be rescinded should his family discover the truth about him.

"It sounds brilliant! When's the test?"

"This afternoon. I wish you could come, but it's a closed set."

"I'll be crossing my fingers for you," I said.

"Thanks! But are you sure you're all right? Sounds like you've got yourself in a spot of bother."

"Oh, it's not so bad. At least the police don't suspect me this time. But I do think they're wrong about the suicide angle."

"And you think you can show them up," Chaz said.

"Not show them up so much as show them the error of their ways. I would hate for this killer to get away with murder."

"Do be careful, old thing. Riding to your rescue in England is one thing. America has its own set of rules."

I laughed. "Don't worry. I'll be careful."

"I forgot to tell you, Varant was asking about you right before I left," Chaz said, voice rife with meaning.

Lord Peter Varant was one of my suitors, for lack of a better word. Rich, titled, and of the highest pedigree, he was a perfect match. Certainly a more acceptable one than Hale Davis. At least according to society. But somehow, we'd never managed to get our act together, so to speak. He'd hint at his interest, then disappear, too busy for anything but a quick note. When meeting in public, I could expect to generally be ignored. Unless, of course, he caught me flirting with someone else. Although the few times we did manage to spend a bit of time together, I found him interesting and incredibly delicious. Frankly, I found it frustrating and terribly annoying.

"What did you tell him?" I asked.

"That you were swanning about America with Butty, of course. He was not amused."

"He hasn't the right to either be amused or not," I said.

"Perhaps you should tell him that," Chaz said archly.

We chatted a bit more, before ringing off. Mindful of the passing time and his need to prepare for the screen test.

By the time we said our goodbyes, I figured it was late enough to ring my villa in France. Mr. Singh picked up on the third ring.

"Yes, Mr. Davis arrived a few minutes ago, Lady Rample. I shall put him on. One moment." I could hear Mr. Singh set the phone down, and then his measured steps as he walked away. Mr. Singh was not one to rush.

I tapped one nail on the desk as I waited impatiently. At last I heard footsteps, quicker than Mr. Singh's measured pacing. Then, "Ophelia."

His voice was low and smooth and just a little husky. It did indecent things to me, and I barely repressed a shiver as goosebumps rose on my arms. I could see his smoldering, bedroom eyes and full, kissable lips as if he were right there with me.

"Hale, how are you?" My voice came out a bit breathier than intended. Which irked me no end. I sounded like Lola when she was playing the sex kitten angle.

"What do you Brits say? Brilliant." He chuckled. "Arrived about a week ago. Already played a few sets down at the club. They really pack in. Standing room only every time."

"That's fantastic!" I'd heard Hale and his band play in London several times at the now defunct Astoria Club. He was so talented. I was glad it was going well. "You think you're going to be there for a while?"

"Another couple months, at least." There was a pause. "You going to make it?"

"Oh, yes. There will just be a slight delay."

Another pause. "Let me guess. You stumbled onto a murder again." There was no censure in his tone, just amusement and perhaps slight exasperation.

"You make it sound like it happens every week."

His laugh was loud and hearty, completely uninhibited. "I'm surprised it's not every day."

"Well, can I help it if I keep getting invited to parties that turn murderous?"

"I suppose not. But you *will* be careful." His voice dipped into a register so sexy I had to grip the phone cord in a vice. "I don't want anything to happen to you."

"I'll be careful," I promised.

"Good. I have plans for you."

Oh, my.

Chapter 11

That afternoon, I found myself back at City Hall. Previously the scene of a strange but joyous occasion, and now here I was trying to get my hands on a suicide note. And for some reason, Lola—probably number one on my suspect list— was actually trying to help me. It made me doubt her place on said suspect list, but I wasn't about to remove her entirely.

Lola was waiting for me in the grand marble foyer. She looked positively smashing in a white V-necked dress with a green circle pattern and matching green velvet bows on the sleeves, at the waist, and marching down the bodice. A little green beret was perched jauntily atop platinum curls, and her pumps and handbag were the same apple green.

"Ophelia, *there* you are. I've been waiting *ages*." Her heels made a clacking sound on the marble floor as she trotted toward me. It didn't escape my notice that her nasally East Coast accent was gone, along with the dropping of her Gs.

"Hello, Lola." I didn't mention that I had arrived at precisely one o'clock as instructed. "Didn't you bring a solicitor?"

"Say what now?" Her brows lowered, then understanding dawned. "Oh, you mean a *lawyer*. No thanks. I've got it covered. Come on." She sashayed across the foyer, and I followed.

We passed through a dizzying array of corridors, archways, and echoing chambers before finally arriving at the part of City Hall inhabited by the Beverly Hills Police Department. A young, earnest-looking man wearing a blue uniform sat perched behind a desk. He nearly fell off his stool when Lola strode in.

"I need to speak with Detective Aarons," she informed him in a loud, carrying voice. "It's *urgent.*"

"Ah... sure. Yes, of course. Right away... M-Miss Burns."

She flashed him a charming smile. "Call me Lola, honey. What's your name?"

"C-Clint." His cheeks flushed crimson. "Clint Anderson."

Lola propped her elbows on his desk. "Well, Clint Anderson, think you can get me an audience with Detective Aarons right away? I'd be sooo grateful."

"Y-yes. I think so." He picked up a telephone receiver, fumbling with it a bit. He finally managed to get it up to his ear and connected with someone. "Visitor for Detective Aarons... No... I don't care if he's busy—this is *urgent!*" He set the receiver down, only dropping it once. "He'll be right up. You can... you could sit over there." He pointed to a row of chairs against the wall.

"Naw, I'll stand," Lola said. "This is my friend, Ophelia. She's a proper English lady. She's got a title and everything. Imagine that."

"How do you do," I said in my proper English lady voice.

Clint barely glanced my way. "Howdy."

"How long you been a policeman, Clint?" Lola fluttered her lashes. I swear she did.

Clint went bright red from his neck all the way to the tips of his ears. "N-not too long. Three years."

"I'm surprised you're not running the place by now. Bet you will be soon enough. You should be in Hollywood, you know that, Clint? With that adorable cleft chin, you could be in the movies."

"Golly, miss, you think so?"

He certainly had the rugged good looks for Hollywood. And if he blushed every time a pretty actress walked by… well, I couldn't imagine he'd do very well as a policeman. Maybe acting would be a good backup plan for him.

While they chatted about screen tests, extras work, gaffers, and I don't know what all, I kept an eye peeled for our elusive detective. At last he put in an appearance.

He pushed through a door next to the front desk and glared at us. His suit was rumpled, his tie askew, and his eyes red rimmed. He'd either been up all night or been on one hell of a bender. I was betting the former since he appeared to take his job quite seriously.

"Miss Burns. Lady Rample. What are you doing here?" His tone was blunt to the point of abject rudeness. I chose to ignore it. Lola did not.

"Is that any way to treat a widow?" she snapped. Then, as if realizing she came off a little less than sympathetic, tears welled up in her big, blue eyes.

Aarons immediately panicked. "There, there, Miss Burns," he said a little desperately. "No need to cry. What can I do for you?"

By this time Lola was sobbing loudly, though strangely enough, her eyes were nearly dry, and her makeup had yet to run. I'm an ugly crier. Lola cried daintily and beautifully. That or she was faking it. Jury was still out on that.

"Miss Burns has a request," I said, taking over since she didn't seem to be in a hurry to answer the man.

Aarons turned to me as if relieved to leave Lola and her sobbing to Clint. "Of course. What can I help you with?"

"The suicide note her husband left. It was written to her, correct?"

"Yes," he said, somewhat hesitantly.

"Well, she never got the chance to see it. It seems only proper she should be allowed to, don't you think? Give her some closure and whatnot."

Aarons rubbed his chin. "I suppose that wouldn't be a problem. It's evidence, of course, so she can't take it with her."

"Of course not," I assured him. "Wouldn't dream of it."

"Well, then, if you ladies would follow me."

Lola immediately quit crying. "Oh, Detective Aarons, you are too kind!"

It was Aarons's turn to blush like a schoolboy. How did she do it?

We followed Aarons through the bullpen teeming with activity and into a tiny but quiet office. He opened a file on the top of the desk and took out a piece of paper, handing it to Lola. "It's been dusted for prints, so go ahead."

"Were there any?" I asked.

He blinked. "Any what?"

"Prints."

"Oh, yes. Cyril's, of course."

"No one else?"

"It's a suicide note, Lady Rample." His tone was a little too sarcastic for my taste. "Why would there be?"

"Just curious," I said lightly. "After all, Carter could have picked it up when he found the body."

"He didn't."

Lola and I bent our heads over the note. It was odd, that note. Not quite... right. For one thing, it looked like it had been torn out of a notebook or journal. The left-hand edge was ragged. For another... it made absolutely no sense.

I dug around in my handbag for my own pencil and notebook and began copying the note word for word. Fortunately, Cyril had wonderful handwriting.

"What are you doing, Lady Rample?" Aarons snapped.

"Copying the note for Lola. That way she can reread it later. It will give her comfort. At least until she can get the original back."

Lola patted my hand and dabbed at her eyes with the white handkerchief in her other hand. "So kind of you, Ophelia. You are a true friend."

Aarons harrumphed, but said nothing more.

The minute I finished copying the note, I tucked my notebook and pencil back in my handbag and gave Lola a nod. She handed the note back to Aarons and thanked him profusely.

"I can rest easier now," she told him.

Aarons eyed us with suspicion, but he had no choice but to escort us out. Just a grieving widow being supported by a friend. Nothing to see here, detective.

But I could feel his eyes boring into my back all the way out of City Hall.

By mutual consent, we waited to discuss Cyril's final letter until we were seated at the restaurant down the street, Café Paradise. It was one of those places with bamboo wallpaper and far too many potted palms, but it appeared popular with the Hollywood set. I saw more than one familiar face. In fact, I was fairly certain that was Gary Cooper in the back-corner dining with a rather attractive blonde.

Once ensconced in a booth, I pulled out my notebook and opened it to the page where I'd copied the note and handed it to Lola.

"Good gosh, Ophelia, your handwriting looks like chicken scratch." Lola squinted at my notebook.

"Well, pardon me, but I was in a hurry. Aarons was looming over us like the Sphinx," I said, spine stiffening.

"I can hardly read it." There was a distinct nasal whine creeping in. A hint of her true self, perhaps? The unpolished girl she'd been before her Hollywood days. I could definitely understand that, though I found her brashness a bit off-putting at times.

"Very well. I shall read it aloud once our food arrives." I took the notebook back.

After the waiter delivered our salads—hearts of romaine with mandarins and melons—I leaned over the note. "This is what he wrote. 'Dearest, Darling...'"

"Cyril never called me that," Lola interrupted with a delicate snort.

"Pardon?" I blinked.

"He called me Lola. Or doll face. Or some ridiculous nonsense. He never called me his 'dearest darling.' I'd've laughed in his face."

"I see. Do you suppose the note was meant for someone else?"

"I don't see who."

"Shall I read the rest?"

She waved languidly and munched on a section of mandarin. "Go on."

"Right. 'It can't be helped. I must do it. It's the only way to make up for what I did to you. I love you. Last night was but a charade'... That's strange."

"What is?"

"Well, I copied down exactly what the note said, right?"

"Sure." She popped another orange section into her mouth.

"So this last line." I tapped the page. "There was no full stop after the last sentence."

She frowned. "What's a full stop?"

"Oh, I believe you Americans call it a period."

Her forehead smoothed out. "Oh, yes. Maybe you just left it off?"

"No," I assured her. "I was very careful to copy it exactly." Knowing it was perhaps a clue, there was no way I would have missed even something so simple as a full stop.

"Well, that's a little strange, right?"

"Yes, it is," I agreed. "It's as if he stopped in the middle of a sentence. He didn't even sign the note. Are you sure he wrote it?"

She nodded. "Positively. It was his hand writing all right."

I guess she would know. "What about the contents of the note? Do they mean something to you?"

"Not a bit." She sipped from her glass of white wine. "He never done me no wrong. He was always the sweetest."

There it was again. That hint of gun moll. "You've no idea to what he could be referring?"

"'Fraid not. I mean, he was sorta doin' me a favor."

I leaned forward, ignoring my own meal. "What do you mean?"

She glanced around to make sure no one was listening, then she lowered her voice. "It ain't common knowledge, see, but Cyril weren't exactly the sort to enjoy the company of women, if you know what I mean."

I did.

She continued. "But we been friends for a couple years, see. And he helped me a lot with my career. So when he asked would I marry him for respectability's sake, I said sure. Why not? Could only be good for my image, right? And he knows everybody who is anybody. Think of the roles I could get."

It made sense. It wasn't that far off from my own marriage. While Felix and I had a genuine fondness for each other, we were never in love. We both provided something the other needed, and it made us happy enough. At least until he kicked the proverbial bucket.

"What about the money he borrowed from you?" I asked, remembering the IOU in Cyril's study.

"How'd you know about that?" she asked suspiciously.

Since I didn't want her to know I'd been snooping, I said, "He told Aunt Butty."

"Oh, well," she waved it off. "He was a little short of funds, see. So I helped him out. I knew he'd pay me back after his next picture. Anyways, he's half the reason I have any money. I kinda owed him."

I mulled over the facts at hand.

1. The note had clearly been torn from some sort of book. Which meant it could have been written at any time. Because why would someone write a suicide note on a piece of paper torn from a random notebook? Surely they would use stationary or something.

2. While the note was written in Cyril's handwriting—per Lola's claim—the note ended abruptly as if he hadn't finished the sentence. Why would he kill himself before finishing whatever it was he wanted to say?

3. It wasn't signed. Who doesn't sign their own suicide note?

4. The note was vague about who it was meant for. Both Carter and Detective Aarons seemed to think it was meant for Lola, but it didn't actually *say* that. I would think that a man about to off himself would want to make sure his final thoughts in this world were delivered to the correct person.

5. Lola had no idea what the note meant. Or so she claimed. I tended to believe her. So, was the note meant for someone else? If so, who was his "Dearest Darling?" To what events did it refer? Who had he done wrong?

So many questions, and so far, the answers were elusive. But from where I sat, I was betting that note had been planted. Perhaps torn from his personal journal, thoughts he'd written down much earlier, but which the real killer felt suited the situation.

I stabbed a chunk of melon and chewed it with vigor, enjoying its sweet, juiciness. That gap in time nagged me.

Why hadn't Carter called the police immediately? There was only one thing for it. I was going to have to force him to tell me. I wasn't sure how yet, but I was convinced Aunt Butty could come up with something. She was devious like that.

I bit into another melon piece with gusto, more convinced than ever that Cyril had been murdered. And I was going to prove it!

Chapter 12

My plan to confront Carter fell apart after we arrived back at the house to find Aunt Butty entertaining guests. She wore a cream pantsuit with a gold kimono trimmed with fringe and gold mules to match. On her head was a turban of peacock blue with a cluster of peacock feathers sticking out from it, all held together with an enormous gold pin in the shape of a peacock. She had a cocktail in one hand and a red cigarette holder in the other, from which dangled an unlit cigarette. Like me, Aunt Butty didn't smoke, but she thought cigarette holders were chic, so she generally had one or two about with which to gesture dramatically.

The guests were Detective Aarons in his cheap suit and an uncomfortable expression, and a freckle-faced uniformed police officer who stood behind Aarons and looked somehow both awkward and eager at the same time.

"Lola! Ophelia! Thank goodness you two are here." Aunt Butty waved the cigarette holder, nearly upsetting a Tiffany art deco lamp.

"Detective," Lola said with an arched brow. "Didn't we just see you?"

He gave her a grim smile. "I'm afraid I had a question that couldn't wait."

"Go on," she said, removing her hat and gloves and fixing herself a drink.

"Do you know this woman?" He held up a snapshot of a middle-aged woman with dark hair and eyes. There was something familiar about her...

Lola gave the picture half a glance. "'Fraid not. Never seen her."

"You sure?" he prodded.

"Of course I am," she snarled. "Whaddya take me for?"

"Wait." Aunt Butty snatched the photo out of Aarons's hand. "I know this woman. This is Dorothea."

"Cyril's ex-wife?" I asked, leaning in for a better look.

"I was Cyril's only wife," Lola snapped, but I noticed a tic near the corner of her left eye. She knew more than she was saying. Question was, how much?

"I know her, too," I said as it finally dawned on me where I'd seen this very same woman. "This is the woman in the bushes."

"The one you told me about?" Aarons asked with a frown. "The one you saw the night of the engagement party?"

I nodded. "The same. I suspected it might be Dorothea but couldn't be sure. Why?"

He plucked the photo from Aunt Butty's fingers. "Because this woman was fished out of the Los Angeles River this morning. Jumper."

"Did she... how is she?" Aunt Butty asked, looking a little pale.

"Dead, I'm afraid," Aarons said gloomily.

"And how did you think to ask us about her?" I asked. "Since I assume you didn't know she was Cyril's ex-wife until now."

"Cyril didn't have any wife but me!" Lola cried again, with a stamp of her foot.

"There, there, dear," Aunt Butty soothed. "There were probably a lot of things about Cyril you didn't know."

"That's not true!"

"Ladies," Aarons said sharply. "To answer your question, Lady Rample, we found her suitcase on the riverbank near where she went in. There was a locket inside with Cyril Brumble's picture and a receipt from a nearby hotel. It was obvious she was connected to Cyril somehow, we just weren't sure how. Hence I decided to ask you ladies." He turned to Aunt Butty. "Do you know anything more about her?"

She shook her head, the peacock feathers waving wildly. "Not much, I'm afraid. Her name is, or rather was, Dorothea Caron. She was originally from France, though I couldn't say where, exactly." She quickly told Aarons what she'd told me earlier about the common law marriage and Dorothea having spent time in a sanitarium.

"This is bull— This is ridiculous!" Lola shouted. "You're making this up!"

"I'm afraid not, dear," Aunt Butty said soothingly, as one might to a recalcitrant child. "Cyril had many years of living before you came along. And he and Dorothea very much lived as man and wife for a number of years."

"But they weren't really married," Lola whined.

"According to the laws of New York, they were," Aunt Butty assured her. "Though, perhaps, not by the laws of California. I'm rather vague on that. In any case, they haven't lived together for quite some time, though I know Cyril has been helping her financially."

"So *that's* where all his money went." Lola's tone was tinged with fury. I could understand that. She'd given Cyril a heck of a lot of money which he'd turned around and given to a woman she had known nothing about. Well, supposedly knew nothing about. I'd be furious, too.

Aarons caught Lola with his sharp gaze. "What do you mean by that, Miss Burns?"

"Nothing," she mumbled. "Just... there were some accounting discrepancies, that's all."

I found that interesting, seeing as how she'd been entirely unconcerned about lending him money. Or so she'd pretended.

"Now I have a headache," Lola said. "If you don't mind, I'm going to go lie down." And without waiting for a dismissal from Aarons, she marched from the room, cocktail in hand.

"Well," Aunt Butty said. Aarons and I nodded in agreement. There wasn't much else to say.

"Anything else you ladies can tell me about this Dorothea Caron?" Aarons asked. "Even the smallest detail could help."

"I'm sorry, Detective, but no. That's all I'm privy to," Aunt Butty said.

I shook my head. "As I told you, I saw her in the bushes the night of the engagement party. She realized she'd been discovered and ran. That's it. You think her death is connected to Cyril's? Like maybe she murdered him and felt so guilty she jumped in the river and drowned herself?"

Aarons looked like he wanted to roll his eyes. Instead, his expression remained stoic. "Cyril Brumble committed suicide. I have no doubt about that. If what your aunt says is true, then Dorothea Caron was an unstable woman. With his support gone, she probably despaired. No more to it than that."

But there was more to it. I was certain of it. "You said you found the receipt for a hotel in her bag. Which hotel?"

He seemed to debate it for a moment. "I guess there's no harm telling you. The Golden Palace Hotel. Low rent sort of place. At least by Hollywood standards. Why do you want to know?"

"Mere curiosity," I said blandly.

Aarons gave me a look that said he didn't believe me. Smart man.

Once Aarons had left, I followed Lola up the stairs and knocked on her bedroom door. "Lola?"

"Come in."

I opened the door to find her seated at her vanity table, repairing her makeup. "Can I ask you something?"

She spun around, eyes wide. "Sure. I guess."

"Why did you want to go shopping with my aunt and me that day? It was so last minute, and you'd only just returned from your honeymoon."

She shrugged. "I'd an outfit planned for a dinner party, but I couldn't find the wrap I wanted to wear with it anywhere. So I figured I'd get a new one. I don't like shopping alone, and since you were here…" She shrugged as if it were the simplest thing in the world and returned to painting her lips.

I eyed her. "Are you certain that's all it was?" I asked, voice rife with suspicion.

"Fine. Cyril and I had a little argument the night before. He was in such a mood. I wanted to avoid him for a while." She puckered up in the mirror. Then, apparently satisfied, tucked her lipstick away in one of the drawers.

"I see." Could that have been the argument the chauffeur overheard? But then he'd been certain the woman wasn't Lola. "What did you argue about?"

Her lips twisted into a sneer. "That's not your business now, is it?" She got up and marched to the open bedroom door. "Please leave. I need to get ready. I've a meeting at the studio to attend."

Giving her a strained smile, I exited the room. I paused and turned around, not sure what I was going to say, but it didn't matter. She slammed the door in my face. Maybe I deserved it, but still, it made me question her innocence. A missing wrap, my ample backside.

I went to find Aunt Butty. She was in the kitchen, commanding Mrs. Mendez who was packing up a large picnic basket.

"Going somewhere?" I asked.

"Yes. We're having an adventure," she informed me.

"What sort of adventure?" I asked, eyeing her with suspicion.

"A picnic at the seaside, naturally. It's nearly time for afternoon tea." Which was when I noticed she was wearing a pair of eye-searing pink and yellow striped beach pajamas. In one hand she clutched a floppy straw hat large enough to act as a sail.

Sea, sand, sun, and food. Plenty of wine, too, judging by the bottles currently wrapped in thick towels. "Sounds delightful, but I must find Carter first. I have some questions for him."

"Carter's not here," the cook informed me. "He has the day off. Went into town early this morning."

"Well, that tears it." I sighed. "I guess I'll go change. Back in a tick, Aunt B." I paused in the doorway. "Mind if we make a stop along the way?"

She lifted a brow. "What sort of stop."

"Little place called the Golden Palace Hotel."

"You minx! No wonder you wormed the hotel name out of Aarons. Go on." She waved me away.

I would have liked to ring Chaz and invite him. This was just the sort of adventure he loved. But I knew he was filming his screen test and didn't want to disturb him.

I quickly changed into my backless one-piece swimming costume. It had a high-necked halter top in navy blue-and-white stripes and a solid navy skirt that just skimmed the tops of my thighs. It was incredibly flattering, but of course one couldn't drive down the road wearing such a thing, so I topped it with a pair of wide beach pajama pants in red with navy trim along the bottom. My sun hat wasn't nearly as impressive as Aunt Butty's but had a jaunty ribbon that matched the pants.

Throwing a few necessities into a bag, I hurried to rejoin Aunt Butty. She was already loaded into the car and urging me to hurry up. "Daylight's wasting, Ophelia!"

The drive was uneventful, and soon Sam was pulling up to a small hotel that had seen better days. The style was hacienda complete with chipped, red-tile roof and peeling cream stucco. The sign was faded and what had once been no doubt lovely grounds were now beds of dried up, overgrown bushes of indeterminate origin.

Inside was not much better. It was clean, which was all that could be said about it, but the floor was worn and creaky, the air stifling and musty, and the scent of boiled cabbage hung heavy. What a depressing place. Why would Dorothea have stayed here? Surely Cyril could have put her up somewhere nicer. Then again, Cyril had been borrowing money from Lola, so maybe he couldn't.

Aunt Butty strode up to the front desk and rapped her knuckles on the warped wood. The plump clerk glanced up, chewing on the corner of his wispy mustache. He actually looked excited to see someone in his lobby.

"Welcome to the Golden Palace. May I help you ladies?" His voice was surprisingly high for such a large man.

"Yes, I think you can," I said, joining my aunt. "You see, a friend of ours is staying here, and we were hoping to visit her, but I simply can't recall which room she was in."

He beamed. "I'll look it up. What's her name?"

"Dorothea Caron," Aunt Butty said.

His face crumpled instantly. "Oh, you haven't heard?"

"Heard what?" I asked, all innocence.

"Miss Caron died the other day." He looked genuinely distraught.

We made the appropriate responses of shock and sadness. "How? What happened?" I asked, still playing my role and hoping he'd offer whatever information he had.

"I'm not sure, but I know the police were here asking about her. Wanted to see her room and all, but she'd already checked out. They said she jumped off a bridge. Suicide."

More gasps. I leaned forward. "But I can see you don't believe that."

He glanced around as if to ensure we were alone. "No, ma'am, I do not. Don't buy it for a hot minute."

Aunt Butty and I exchanged meaningful glances. "Really? Why?"

He leaned closer. "Well, thing is you see, she got a call that night. The night they say she jumped. Took it right here." He pointed at the black telephone perched on the counter. "She was going to stay another night, but instead she told me to get her bill ready, then went and packed her things."

"I wonder who called her?" Aunt Butty asked the ether.

He shrugged. "Couldn't say. All I know is it was a man's voice on the line. He asked for her by name."

So someone who knew who she was and knew where she was staying. "Did he know her room number?"

The young man shook his head. "After she returned to the lobby to pay her bill, I asked her about it. It was late, you see, and it didn't seem right—a lady going out in the middle of the night by herself. Asked if I could get her a cab."

"And what did she say?" I prodded.

"She thanked me, but said she'd walk. The river wasn't far."

"River?" I asked.

"Los Angeles River. It's a short walk from here," he said.

"But why would she walk to the Los Angeles River in the middle of the night?" Aunt Butty wondered. "Odd thing to do, if you ask me."

"Beats me," the clerk said. "When I told her it was dangerous, she said not to worry. She was meeting a friend."

Meeting a friend at the very place where she supposedly jumped off a bridge and died. After receiving a phone call from an unknown man. How very mysterious. I had a bad feeling that whoever Dorothea's friend was, was no friend at all, but a blood thirsty killer!

After we'd thanked the hotel clerk and got back in the car, Sam drove us to a lovely sandy beach. For an afternoon in the middle of the week, the place was surprisingly crowded. Still, Sam found a place to park and escorted us and our picnic basket down to the waterfront. He laid out a blanket, set up a massive umbrella, then told us he'd wait for us at the car. Seemed a shame for him to be stuck in the car on such a lovely day, but then everyone seemed to think we were a little crazy, wanting a day at the beach.

"This isn't at all what I expected," Aunty Butty said, squinting down the coastline with disapproval. "What are those ghastly things?"

I glanced in the direction she was staring. She wasn't wrong. This wasn't how I'd imagined the coast of California would look like. In the distance, up and down the beach marched rows upon rows of black, wrought iron towers stretching their ugly lengths into the sharp blue sky.

"They're oil derricks," I told her.

"Beastly things. Why on earth would they put them here? What do they do?"

"Pull oil up out of the ground. For powering motorcars and that sort of thing."

"Well someone should burn them down. All of them."

"I'm fairly certain that would be illegal," I said dryly.

"Having them here should be illegal. They're an eyesore," Aunt Butty said, opening one of the bottles of wine while I set out Mrs. May's feast. There were slices of cold ham between brown bread slathered with mustard, a rather odd concoction called potato salad, pickles, stuffed eggs, fresh apricots, a thermos of hot coffee, and graham cracker cake. I must admit the last one was beyond divine.

We rushed through our picnic. Not only because of the ugliness of the oil rigs, but also because everyone kept staring at us like we were mice in a cage. It was... unsettling. I suppose they weren't used to seeing the upper crust on their beach.

The minute we were done, we packed up without waiting for Sam and struggled back through the sand, dragging the umbrella. The wind had changed and there was the distinct smell of burning oil wafting our way. It made my nose itch.

At last we made it to the car, but our driver was nowhere to be seen.

"Where do you suppose he got to?" Aunt Butty asked.

"He couldn't have got far," I said. "Not without the car." I stood on tiptoes and craned my neck to peer over the sea of parked automobiles. "I see some men playing a dice game. I bet he's over there. I'll go get him."

"Very well. I'll go with you." Aunt Butty set down the picnic basket and adjusted her hat.

"You should wait here," I argued. "Guard our things."

"They aren't *our* things, Ophelia. And no one is going to steal them. An old umbrella and an empty picnic basket? Don't be absurd. I'm going with you." I recognized that steely glint in her eye. There'd be no budging her. "I want to give that chauffeur a piece of my mind. He should have waited for us by the car."

I sighed. "Very well."

I marched toward the game, Aunt Butty hot on my heels. I'd only gone a few paces when a man stepped out in front of me. He wore a brown suit with little white stripes running through it. He had a face like a hatchet and little rat eyes that gave me a distinctly unpleasant feeling.

"Pardon me," I said in my most imperious voice.

"Don't think so," he said, giving me a once-over with those cold eyes.

My dander went up. "Move at once!" I commanded.

"Or what?" he asked, crossing his arms and cocking his head just a little to the right.

I'd have liked to have given him a sock in the eye, but Aunt Butty grabbed my arm. "Ophelia." Her voice held a note of warning.

"What is it?"

"Look behind you."

I glanced over my shoulder to see two more men standing behind us. One was very large, his belly straining at his white button-down shirt. He wore no suit jacket—appalling—and had huge patches of damp under his arms. He glared at me from under the brim of his fedora. Next to him was a slightly shorter man, but equally broad, only with muscle instead of fat. My stomach gave a flutter of unease. I turned back to Hatchet Face.

"What is the meaning of this?"

"Our boss would like to have a word with you, Lady Rample."

"How do you know my name?" I demanded. My feelings of unease grew apace.

He leered. "I have my ways. Now come along and no one gets hurt."

"Oh, I've heard that before," Aunt Butty huffed. "If you think we're going with you, you've got another think coming, my good sir!"

Hatchet Face sighed. "Bring them."

And before we could so much as let out a scream, we'd been gagged, tied, and thrust into the back of a black sedan.

Chapter 13

The black sedan drove for what seemed like ages, wending its way along the coast. Flashes of ocean blue peeped through the bristle of oil rigs that marched up and down in neat rows like soldiers. On the other side of the road, dry, brown hills stretched up into harsh, blue sky. Here and there a villa surrounded by greenery poked out from a cliff as if trying to grasp the sea.

I tried to enjoy the view, such as it was, and not focus on what fate awaited us, but it was impossible. I may or may not have an overly dramatic imagination. I conjured up any number of dastardly possibilities.

Perhaps they were white slavers who were going to sell us to a desert sheik! I tried to imagine white slavers wanting Aunt Butty. My imagination failed me. Fine. Not white slavers.

Gangsters who thought we'd stolen their money. Why would gangsters think we'd stolen their money? The closest I'd ever come to a real-life gangster was when Lola opened her mouth.

Hatchet Face had said his boss wanted to speak to us. Could it be that ghastly movie man who'd told me to lose weight? Surely not. Why would he send goons after me at the beach of all places?

Could they be G-men? Sent by the government to... what? Perhaps they wanted to hold us for ransom? Or murder us! Surely American government agents didn't do such things.

I was getting rather nonsensical. And I was running out of ideas. Also, I was starting to work myself into a lather. I took a few deep, calming breaths and told myself not to be a ninny.

The car pulled up in front of what was clearly a nightclub. A large neon sign, unlit in the middle of the day, proclaimed it to be the Monte Carlo. I'd been to the actual Monte Carlo. Trust me, it looked nothing like this rather dodgy, windowless brick building.

We were ushered inside, still gagged and with our hands tied in front of us. Frankly, it was humiliating. Where were the police when you needed them?

The two big men were left to guard the door while Hatchet Face pushed us ahead of him into the main room of the club itself. To my right, along the longest wall, was a well-stocked bar. Funny, that. Didn't they have prohibition out west? To the left against that wall were several plush booths. To the front was a low stage, no doubt for musicians and such. And ringing the dance floor in front of the stage were about a dozen small tables with chairs.

One of the booths was occupied by a lone man. He looked to be late thirties or early forties. Handsome, but in a gone-to-seed sort of way. His features had turned fleshy rather than defined, and there was a bit of extra padding around his middle. A gold pinky ring flashed in the dim overhead light. He was eating a rather large platter of steak and eggs, and there was a substantial cocktail at his elbow.

"Hey, Boss. Brung the ladies like you asked," Hatchet Face said, shoving us forward so hard, Aunt Butty stumbled. If only my hands were free and I had my handbag with me. I'd do to Hatchet Face what I'd done to that Louis person.

The boss looked from Hatchet Face to us and back again. "You tied them up?" His voice was surprisingly cultured and very irritated. "What were you thinking, you palooka?"

"Sorry, Boss, but they got a little feisty."

Boss set down his knife and fork and rubbed his forehead as if he suddenly had a headache. "Remove their gags and ropes. Immediately." His voice was perfectly calm, but there was something deadly in his eyes. Like a snake that just spotted his dinner. I shuddered, but inwardly. Wasn't going to let him or his flunkies see.

Hatchet Face released Aunt Butty first. She spat out her gag, quivering with fury. "Well, I never!"

"Is this how you treat ladies?" I demanded the moment I was free. "I'll have you know we are visitors to your shores. We are members of the British aristocracy! Never in my life have I been treated in such a fashion!"

"I'll have you know I'm acquainted with the governor!" Aunt Butty all but shouted. I tried very hard to keep my expression bland. I knew very well that Aunt Butty had no idea who the governor of California was. "I will tell him just exactly what sort of treatment I received from your... goons."

A tiny smile quirked Boss's lip. "I do apologize ladies. My *goons* had very specific instructions, which they obviously ignored. They'll be dealt with."

I swear, Hatchet Face wilted.

"Please," Boss said, waving to the empty benches on either side of him, "be seated, ladies. Can I interest you in a beverage?"

"If it's got alcohol, then yes," Aunt Butty said, heaving herself into the booth.

I nodded, sliding in across from her. "Please."

He lifted a hand in the air and snapped his fingers imperiously. Within seconds, a uniformed waiter had appeared, and cocktail glasses were slid in front of us. I eyed the pale greenish liquid with suspicion.

"Southside," Boss informed us. "Simple, but refreshing, don't you think?" He took a sip, and we followed.

It was, indeed, surprisingly delicious, and as he said, refreshing. Slightly sweet, with a tang of lime and just a hint of mint. I certainly would not be unhappy should this be added to my repertoire of favorite beverages.

"I'm not usually a gin person," I told him, "but this is quite nice. Now who the devil are you?"

He lifted a single brow, and I noticed there was a white scar running through it. It made him look equal parts rakish and dangerous.

"Vincent Montano, but you can call me Vinnie."

"Charmed, I'm sure," Aunt Butty said dryly. "Now what is the meaning of this? Sending your goons after us. Positively shocking behavior." She downed her cocktail in one go and held out her empty glass. Sure enough, the waiter appeared, whisked away the glass and replaced it with a new, icy cold cocktail. "I assure you, the British Embassy will hear about this. I'll have you know I'm very close friends with Sir Ronald Lindsay."

I had no idea if this was true or not. With Aunt Butty, anything was possible. She could have very easily met the Ambassador to the United States during her various travels and adventures. Then again, she could be lying through her teeth. It was impossible to tell. Either way, Vinnie appeared unconcerned.

"No need for that," Vinnie assured her, spreading his hands. "We're just having a conversation."

"Sure. One in which we were bound and gagged and forced into a motorcar," I said dryly.

"Yes. My men were... overzealous."

Aunt Butty snorted and drained her second cocktail. At this rate she'd be potted before supper time.

"Listen," Vinnie folded his hands and leaned forward as if wanting to impart some great secret, "I wanted to chat with you about Lola."

I blinked. "Lola?"

"Lola Burns. You know, the actress. You're staying with her."

"And what do you have to do with Miss Burns?" Aunt Butty's tone could have given a snowman frostbite.

"Nothin.' Nothin.' We're just good pals, you see?" He leaned back and gave us a bland smile.

"No, I don't see," I said. "You don't exactly strike me as the sort of person who cavorts with film stars."

"Oh," he said, propping his elbows on the table and leaning toward me. "Who *do* you see me cavorting with?"

Aunt Butty smacked him with her folding fan. Right across the back of the head. I didn't even know she had a fan on her person. "That will be quite enough from you, young man."

Vinnie held up a hand. "Apologies, ladies. Put that thing away, Willy."

That's when I realized Hatchet Face had pulled out a pistol. Good gosh. I swear I broke out in a cold sweat.

"Please, ladies, hear me out." Vinnie held his hands up. "Truth is, I'm concerned."

"About?" It was my turn to lift a brow.

"Lola doesn't need her name being dragged through the mud, see?"

"Why would Lola's name be dragged through the mud?" Aunt Butty asked.

"Well, you ladies are sort of stirring things up. Making waves. Asking uncomfortable questions." He made a waffling motion with his hand.

"Uncomfortable for the murderer, maybe," I muttered.

He thrust his index finger at me. "This is what I'm talking about. That husband of hers wasn't murdered. It was suicide, see."

"I don't think so," I insisted. "There is evidence that points directly to murder."

"What evidence? Never mind. I don't wanna know. What I want you to do is back off."

Aunt Butty sucked in air. "Well, really! I never!"

"I have to agree with my aunt. That's terribly cheeky of you." I could think of a stronger word, but Vinnie Montano didn't seem like the kind of person I wanted to cross.

"I'm just askin.' As a favor. Back off. Let the police do their job."

"Sure. We can do that," I lied through my teeth.

"Good. Good." He looked pleased with himself. "Now we've got that straight. Willy will drive you home." He gave Willy the stink eye. "With all due deference. These here are elegant ladies."

"Sure, Boss. Whatever you say."

"By the way," I said as we stood to leave. "What's Lola to you?"

I thought he wasn't going to answer at first, but then he said, "Let's just say we were very close once and leave it at that." His tone told me that further questions would be unwelcome. His cold eyes had me thinking of sleeping and fishes.

Chapter 14

"Good gosh, Lola dated a mobster," Aunt Butty declared once we were safe back at the house and ensconced in the living room with restorative cocktails. As if Aunt Butty needed more cocktails to restore her. "Who'd have guessed it."

I couldn't say I was that surprised. Every now and then, something slipped into Lola's speech patterns. Something that proved she wasn't the wide-eyed innocent she wanted the world to see. Lola had a past, and it was darker than anyone suspected. "I guess I can tick 'get kidnapped by gangsters' off my to-do list," I said.

"Don't be flippant, Ophelia. They could have easily murdered us."

"Could have but didn't." I was completely convinced Vinnie Montano was perfectly capable of murder when it suited him. I was also convinced he wasn't the sort to murder people willy nilly for no good reason. I hoped.

"What are we going to do?" she asked.

"I suppose we must stop investigating." I eyed her closely to see how she felt about it.

"Nonsense! I'm not having some two-bit mobster telling me what to do." Clearly, she'd been watching American gangster films again. "No, we will continue with our inquiries. We'll just have to be cautious about what we do, especially where Lola is involved. What's next on the agenda?"

"I'd like to confront Lola about Vinnie Montano, but that will have to wait until she gets home." When we'd arrived back at the house, we'd discovered Lola had taken off again. A party or some such. "And since I haven't been able to question the butler, I suppose we could search his room for clues."

"Excellent." She heaved herself to her feet. "Let's go."

Carter's room was off the back of the kitchen through the butler's pantry. It was a small room, impeccable, nearly Spartan. There was a simple wood framed single bed, a matching nightstand and dresser, and plain white cotton curtains on the tiny window. A small door led into a doll-sized closet. The only item of excitement was a framed photograph next to the bedside table. I picked it up, expecting to see the photo of a woman. Or perhaps a family. Instead…

"Oh, crikey. Look at this." I handed the photo to my aunt.

"What is the butler doing with a picture of Cyril?"

"I think maybe they were, er… close," I said.

She gave me a look. "Don't be such a prude, Ophelia." She peered at the image. "Anything is possible, I suppose."

"Likely, I'd say." I took the photograph back and replaced it exactly as it had been. No sense broadcasting our visit. "Let's check the closet."

The closet was more as less as expected. A row of hangers marched neatly along a hanging rod. From each hung a meticulously pressed item of clothing: black trousers, black jackets, black waistcoats, white shirts. "No surprises here."

"No casual clothing for his day off?" Aunt Butty asked.

"Maybe he's wearing them." I pointed to two empty hangers.

"Perhaps." She propped her hands on her ample hips. "What is he up to, do you suppose?"

"I don't know." I stretched to feel along the shelf at the top of the closet. Nothing. And then, at the very back I brushed a bit of cloth. Snagging a corner, I pulled it out and held it up.

It was a white evening wrap embroidered with gold and silver threads. Very feminine.

"That isn't Carter's," Aunt Butty said dryly. "I'd put good money on it."

"No, I think this is Lola's missing wrap. The one she had to rush out to replace. And look."

I held the wrap up to the window. It was peppered with holes, each one singed around the edges. Black stippling radiated from some of the holes and there was the distinct odor of smoke and cordite.

"Well, I never," Aunt Butty gasped. "Those are bullet holes!"

"Actually, it's probably a single bullet hole. Probably the wrap was wadded up when the bullet passed through it," I said.

"What are the two of you doing here?"

We both whirled to find the butler glaring at us. He tried to snatch the wrap from my hands, but I yanked it away.

"This is Miss Burns's. What are you doing with it?" He demanded.

That startled me. "I know it's Lola's. Why was it in *your* closet? And why are there bullet holes in it?"

"I have no idea why it's here," he said. "Or why there are bullet holes in it. As you well know, I don't lock my room. Anyone could have put it in here. For all I know, you put it here."

"Why ever would she do that?" Aunt Butty demanded.

"I don't know. All you rich people are crazy. Now give me that wrap so I can return it to Miss Burns."

I tucked it behind me. "No, thanks. I think I'm going to give it to Detective Aarons. I'm sure he'll be very interested."

At the mention of Aarons, he hesitated. "Do as you like," he snarled. "Now get out of my room."

We rushed from his room, not stopping until we were safely locked in my room. "I'm certain this wrap was used to muffle the gunshot that killed Cyril."

"I believe you're correct."

"Carter's right," I admitted. "Anyone could have put this wrap in his room."

"Could someone be trying to frame him?" Aunt Butty asked, dropping into the chair near the window. "Lola, for instance. It's her wrap, after all."

"Maybe." I perched on the edge of the bed. "Although she seems smarter than to use her own clothing."

Aunt Butty frowned. "I suppose Dorothea could have done it. She'd have had good reason to want to frame Lola."

"Good point," I agreed. "What we need is more evidence."

"Or a confession," Aunt Butty pointed out. "Although if Dorothea did it, that boat has sailed."

"As if we're going to get a confession out of either Lola or Carter." I thought it over. "What we need is a motive."

"Well, Lola's motive is pretty obvious, don't you think? She'll inherit everything."

"Not much to inherit," I said. "While I was searching Cyril's study, I found paperwork. Bank statements. That sort of thing. He's dead broke. In fact, he owed her money."

Her eyes widened. "Really? I had no idea."

I nodded. "He hasn't made a film in a while. And he's been living well beyond his means for years. Looks like he's been borrowing from Peter to pay Paul. Even borrowing from Lola. If anything, her motive was to get rid of someone who was sponging her dry. After all, she got what she wanted from him. A leg up in her career."

Aunt Butty nodded thoughtfully. "She's already well on her way to the top. Right. So Carter. What could his motive possibly be?"

"I think Carter was in love with Cyril," I mused. "Whether it was mutual, it's hard to say. But there is the photograph by his bed, and that argument I heard between the two of them. Although from what I overheard, it sounded like Cyril was angry with Carter for spending time with someone else. What if they were having a relationship that went wrong? Or maybe Carter wanted a relationship. Was jealous of Lola. And then there's Dorothea. I suppose her motive could have been jealousy. That Cyril left her for Hollywood and then another woman."

"It's all speculation. We're going to need more if we're going to take this to that Detective Aarons."

"I know." I sighed, staring down at the twisted ball of fabric in my hands. "I'm just not sure how or where to find it."

"The note. You said it came from a journal or a notebook. Maybe we could find the original book it was torn from. Then we'd have our proof."

I nodded. "Yes, but it could easily have been destroyed by now. Still, it doesn't hurt to look. Let's scour the house top to bottom."

"After supper, dear. I'm ravenous."

Chapter 15

Over supper, we formulated a battle plan.

"We already searched the butler's room, and you've covered the study," Aunt Butty said, waving around a forkful of roast beef with horseradish sauce before popping it into her mouth. Once she'd chewed thoroughly she continued. "I suggest we continue with the main floor, then work our way upward."

"And if someone wants to know what we're doing?"

"We're lost looking for the loo," she said, as if it were the most obvious thing. "Lola's out again. Studio, probably. That woman spends more time at the studio. I swear she has a lover."

"Which would give her an excellent motive for murder," I murmured. And it would ensure we could safely search the house without her knowing. Mrs. Mendez was out. The chauffeur was busy doing whatever he did with the cars in the garage. Of course, there was still Carter to contend with, but I was fairly certain we could keep out of his way.

I nibbled at a lemon biscuit. The cook had called them "cookies." Whatever they were, they were delicious. I helped myself to another.

"Hopefully we'll find something in the house. If not, I suppose we'll have to move to the grounds."

Aunt Butty groaned. "We'll never find anything in that jungle. Let's cross our fingers and pray something pops up." She dusted off her hands. "Right. I'll start in the kitchen. Why don't you start here in the dining room?"

With supper finished, Aunt Butty departed for the kitchen, while I took a slow turn around the dining room. Despite being almost crammed to the gills, there weren't many places one could hide a book, even a small journal. The dining room was almost petite, with a table that sat twelve at most. On one side of the room was an antique sideboard. On the other, a matching china hutch. In each corner sat either a potted fern, or a velvet armchair. Oil paintings portraying medieval scenes hung from the walls. Other than the table and chairs, there were no other pieces of furniture, and the hutch was fronted in glass, which meant one couldn't hide so much as a button in it. That left the sideboard.

It was one of those tall, Edwardian monstrosities, made of walnut with mirrors everywhere. There were but two small cupboard doors behind which one could conceal something. They opened easily to reveal what one might expect: extra cloth napkins, napkin rings, a neatly folded table cloth, and so on. I checked between the folds of cloth but found nothing concealed. The dining room was out.

I repeated my search in the living room, with almost equal results. Other than a playing card beneath the sofa and a couple of coins wedged behind the cushions, there was nothing of interest concealed anywhere in the room.

Aunt Butty popped her head through the door. "Any luck?"

"No. You?"

"Not unless you count the gossip magazines I found hidden in the pantry. Mrs. Mendez has a frivolous side I never expected."

I sighed. "Bedrooms next, I suppose."

We climbed the stairs slowly.

"We already searched Cyril's room," Aunt Butty said. "So have the police."

I nodded. "And we know there's nothing in our rooms. That leaves Lola's room and the spare room. I'll take Lola's."

"If you insist."

Aunt Butty disappeared into the spare room. Getting into Lola's room proved more difficult. The door was locked. I smirked. As if that would ever keep me out.

Chaz had taught me the fine art of lock-picking. I'd no idea where he'd picked it up, but I found it came in handy. Within minutes, I was standing inside the purple-walled sanctuary that was Lola's domain. It smelled so strongly of roses and French powder, I sneezed.

Where to start? I checked under the bed and between the mattress, not expecting to find much and not disappointed when I didn't. Her closet and drawers also proved a bust. So I sat down at her vanity which was littered with pots of creams, vials of perfumes, tins of powder, and enough cosmetics to supply an entire chorus line of Parisian burlesque dancers.

I picked up a pot of cold cream and removed the lid, giving it a sniff. The smell was heavenly. Cocoa butter with just a touch of something woodsy and a hint of orange flower. Delightful. I made a mental note of the label and decided I would pick some up before I headed back to England. Or rather, to my villa in France.

Screwing the lid back on, I replaced the pot exactly as I found it, label out. There were also pots of rose pomade and vanishing cream, all with attractive labels neatly lined up.

The vanity had small drawers on either side. I slid out the one on the left. Inside were even more pots, tins, vials, and tubs. My word, the woman had a cosmetics addiction. A quick search proved there was nothing else to be found. Not that I'd expected much. Though it would have been interesting to find a pile of love letters, say from Sam the chauffeur. I smiled, remembering that he had a bit of a crush on "the Mrs," though I doubted Lola would give him the time of day. I slid the drawer shut and turned my attention to the one on the right.

That drawer held handkerchiefs. A soft, fluffy pile of white cotton and linen squares edged in silk and lace or covered in neat little embroidery stitches. I ruffled through them until my fingers hit something solid and smooth. Nothing at all like the handkerchiefs. Pulling them aside, I lifted the rectangular object out.

It was a small notebook, not much bigger than the length of my hand, bound in leather. I opened the cover and on the inner page was written "C. Brumble."

"Crikey," I mumbled. "It's Cyril's notebook." Sure enough, as I flipped through, I found page after page of intimate thoughts and feelings in Cyril's neat handwriting. He never named names, but there were effusive protestations of love and devotion side-by-side with long, despairing rants against the cruelty of the world and of love. And right in the middle of the book were the ragged remains of a missing page.

I slammed the drawer shut and bolted from the room, yelling for Aunt Butty. She popped her head out of the spare room. "Whatever is the matter? Did you find another body?"

"No! Even better." I brandished the book. "I found Cyril's journal. The one the killer used to fake the suicide note."

"Huzzah!" Aunt Butty cried. "We should ring Aarons up straight away. He's going to want to know about this and the wrap with the bullet hole."

She was right. We went straight to Cyril's study and the telephone. Within moments we were put through to Aarons.

Once I was finished with my explanations, I waited for him to say something. When he remained silent, I prodded. "Well? You know what this means, right?"

He sighed heavily. "It means that Cyril Brumble was murdered."

"Yes!" Finally.

"I'm going to send a man around to collect the evidence from you. He'll be there in half an hour. Don't go anywhere."

"Of course not," I assured him. "What are you going to do?"

"I'm going to go down to the movie studio and arrest Lola Burns for murdering her husband."

Chapter 16

"Oh, this is awful, just awful," I said, pacing back and forth across the study carpet.

"Isn't this what we wanted? For Aarons to admit it was murder and arrest someone?" Aunt Butty asked.

"Of course, but I wanted him to arrest the *right* person."

"And you don't think Lola is the right person?"

I sighed and dropped into the desk chair. "I don't know. I can't be sure."

"Let's look at the facts." It was Aunt Butty's turn to pace as she ticked off each item on her fingers. "One. As dubiously effective as it may have been, Lola's wrap was used in an attempt to muffle the shot that killed Cyril."

I nodded. There was no arguing that. "Correct. Although it probably wasn't needed since the gun was a small caliber and wouldn't have made much noise."

"Possibly an inexperience gunman, then?"

"Possibly," I agreed.

"Two. The journal from which the killer tore a page to use as a fake suicide note was found in Lola's vanity table in her locked bedroom."

"Yes." No arguing that, either.

"Three. Lola had more than one motive to murder her husband. He was likely having an affair with another man, *and* he was broke, likely sponging off her."

"Also true."

"Finally, while she may have claimed to be asleep at the time of death, in reality, she has no alibi for the time of the murder, and her behavior afterward was highly suspicious."

I groaned. "All true."

"So why do you doubt Lola is the killer? Who else do you think did it?"

"Honestly?" I said. "I think the butler did it."

Her eyes widened. "A bit cliché but go on."

"We found Lola's wrap in his room."

"His unlocked room," she reminded me. "As he pointed out, anyone could have planted the wrap in his room any time after the murder."

"Yes, but that could equally be said about the journal in Lola's room."

"Except her door is locked."

"Right," I admitted. "But I was able to pick the lock. And he's the butler. He's probably got a skeleton key."

"Oh. I hadn't thought of that." She sat down in the other chair and tapped her cheek. "What about motive?"

"Well, if he was having an affair with Cyril, then jealousy?"

She frowned. "Not sure that's good enough. After all, they could easily continue having an affair right under Lola's nose. I mean, he works here for heaven's sake. And I'm not sure Lola would have even cared as long as they were discreet about it."

"Well, what about the argument I overheard?" I said. "It could be that Carter was cheating on Cyril. Cyril threatened to fire him and even though he didn't in the end, Carter could have been worried it was only a matter of time."

"Except that killing Cyril was a good way to murder himself out of a job," Aunt Butty pointed out. "There was no way he could be sure Lola would keep him on."

Male voices suddenly echoed in from the entry hall. I couldn't quite hear what was being said, so I got up and slipped over to the study door, cracking it open, I put one eye to the crack. Sam and Carter were standing in the middle of the hall arguing.

"No can do, man," Sam said. "I've got to pick up Miss Burns in an hour. Don't have time to be running your ass around. Why don't you call a taxi?"

Obviously, they hadn't yet heard Lola was being arrested.

"I don't have time to call a taxi. I need to get into town immediately," Carter snapped.

"Don't know what to tell you." The chauffeur held up his hands.

"Very well. I shall take the Roadster." Carter marched purposefully toward the garage.

"Oh, no, you don't." Sam started after him, but I grabbed him by the sleeve.

"Let him go," I whispered. "We need to follow him."

"I can't let him drive the Roadster. Lola'll have my head. And we can't follow him. I need to pick her up."

"The police are arresting Lola for murder as we speak," Aunt Butty informed him.

"Is that true?" He turned to me with wide eyes.

"Yes, it is." I was quite sure he had a crush on Lola, which played into my plans perfectly. "So if you value her life, you will do exactly what I say. Let Carter go, and then we'll follow him."

He hesitated only a moment before giving a brief nod. "The Rolls is out front."

We dashed down the hall and out onto the drive. Sure enough, the Rolls stood gleaming beneath the afternoon sun. Sam slid behind the steering wheel, while Aunt Butty and I crammed into the back yelling, "Go! Go!"

"Uh, there's no point in going," Sam pointed out. "He's just barely pulling out of the garage. See?"

I leaned forward to peer through the windscreen—windshield, since we were in America. Sure enough, through the trees I caught sight of the garage, a glimmer of red slowly moving from it.

"For a man in a hurry, he sure drives like a slowpoke," Aunt Butty said.

Which was rich, coming from her. She never ceased to complain about the speediness of my driving. I'll have you know I'm an excellent driver. I just like to get places in a hurry.

We waited with a great deal of impatience as Carter slowly backed the Roadster out of the garage and inched up the drive. Once the Roadster was out of sight around a curve, Sam gunned the Rolls's engine and took off after him. As we rounded the bend, the Roadster was just pulling out onto Easton Drive.

Sam sped up to catch him, only to discover that Carter was moving at a snail's pace along the narrow street. Not that I blamed him. Hedges and high stone walls crowded the sides of the road, making it almost impossible avoid a head-on collision with anyone coming from the opposite direction.

"Don't let him see us," Aunt Butty ordered.

"Yes, ma'am," Sam replied with a cheeky grin, angling his cap over one eye. He was kind enough not to point out he was already doing a bang-up job.

At last we turned left onto Benedict Canyon Drive. I admit to giving a sigh of relief as the road widened and the traffic picked up, making it easier to follow Carter and less likely we'd end up in someone's front garden.

We wound down through the hills until finally arriving at Santa Monica Boulevard which we then followed straight into Hollywood. Carter never looked back once, clearly intent on reaching wherever he was going.

"I think he's headed to that hotel up there," Sam said, pointing to the large, art deco structure glowing in the sun. Lush palm trees and jacarandas—those strange trees with the gorgeous purple flowers—surrounded the hotel, lending it a sense of exotic elegance.

Sure enough, Carter pulled into the drive, got out of the Roadster, grabbed his case, and handed his keys to the valet before slipping inside. Once he was out of sight, Sam pulled up behind him.

"I'll go in with you," he offered.

"No, no. You stay with the vehicle," I said. "We can handle this, can't we, Aunt Butty?"

"If you say so," she said somewhat doubtfully.

"We're just going to spy on him, nothing more," I insisted, marching into the lobby.

It was a lovely lobby, luxurious and new with a fountain full of cherubs smack dab in the middle. Carter was nowhere to be seen. So I marched straight up to the register and gave the uniformed man my most imperious look. "A gentleman just came through here. Black suit. Carrying a brown case. Which room is he in?"

He gave me an equally imperious look. "We at the St. John Hotel are not in the habit of giving out information on our guests."

Aunt Butty snorted. "He's no guest. He couldn't afford this place. He's a butler."

The man's eyes widened. "A-a what?"

"Butler," I confirmed. "Nothing wrong with it, of course. Honest profession and all that, but certainly not one that allows him to pay your fees. Unless he's not a guest. Maybe he's visiting someone?"

He seemed to recover, puffing out his chest. "I'm afraid I'm not at liberty to say."

Bingo. "Tell us which room, or I start screaming."

"Go ahead," said Mr. Smug, crossing his arms over his chest. "You'll just make a fool of yourself."

Clearly, he didn't know me. I could give two figs for what anyone thought. I opened my mouth, only to have Aunt Butty interrupt.

"Listen, young man. I know people. People in Hollywood. People who can crush you like a bug. Or..." she leaned over the desk, catching his eye. As if against his will, he swayed toward her, almost hypnotized.

"Or?" he asked.

"Or they can give you exactly what you want. A shot at the silver screen."

I stared from my aunt to the scrawny hotel employee with the bug-eyes and protruding Adam's apple. No way was *he* silver screen material. But, of course, my aunt had only a passing acquaintance with the truth when it suited her, and she'd a way of making people believe whatever she was telling them. Clearly, he did.

"Room 182," he said, eyes wide, almost hypnotized. "Second floor."

"Very good. Key?" she held out her gloved hand, into which he placed a brass key. "Thank you, dear. What's your name?"

"Vernon."

"Vernon. Very good. My people will call your people. Come, Ophelia!" And she sailed from the lobby, Vernon staring after us, shell-shocked.

I followed her, feeling a bit shell-shocked, myself. She took no notice, heading up the wide staircase toward what the Americans oddly referred to as the second floor.

She didn't bother knocking but used the key to unlock the door before flinging it open, announcing, "A-ha!"

A-ha, indeed. For beyond the door we found Carter in an amorous embrace.

"Crikey," I muttered. "Is that?"

"Wayne Palmer?" Aunt Butty said in stentorian tones. "I believe it is."

"Good lord." I couldn't stop staring. I'd seen Wayne Palmer on many a movie screen back home. He was one of the hottest young stars out there. Known far and wide as a ladies' man. Certainly not who I'd expect to see lip-locked with Cyril's butler.

"Who are you?" Wayne Palmer demanded. His face was dead white, and he looked like he might keel over.

"Ophelia, Lady Rample," I said, striding forward with outstretched hand, "and my aunt, Lady Lucas. We're guests of Cyril Brumble and Lola Burns. We've met. At the pool party."

Wayne went whiter, if that were possible, and without another word, he bolted past us, out the door. I didn't bother following him. He wasn't important.

"So cheating on Cyril, were you Carter?" I asked, turning to the other man. His face was positively persimmon with anger. I took a stab in the dark. "Is that why he fired you?"

"You and your nosy aunt need to butt out," he snarled.

"Or?"

"Or I'll make you." He rushed toward me, knocking Aunt Butty aside, and grabbing me around the throat.

At first, I was so startled, I couldn't move. But then breathing became an issue, so I clawed at his face, digging my nails in and dragging bloody furrows down his cheek. He smacked me across the face hard enough to make my ears ring. So I kneed him in the soft bits. Except he moved at just the right moment and I hit his thigh instead.

Somewhere in the background, I could hear Aunt Butty shouting. I wished she'd do something more... productive. It was getting rather hard to breathe.

I went for his eyes—those angry, piggy eyes—but he jerked away before I could cause any real harm. I stomped on his insole and he howled in rage and pain before smacking me again.

And then there was a godawful clanging crash, Carter's eyes went wide, then they rolled back in his head as he slid to the floor. Aunt Butty stood over him with a triumphant smile, clutching a telephone to her ample bosom. "Never let it be said these things aren't good for something."

I touched my throat which felt sore and raw. "I don't think anyone's ever said that." My voice was hardly more than a croak.

Before she could answer, the room was suddenly swarmed with policemen. They stopped in the middle of the room and stared about them in confusion, muttering to each other about who they should or should not arrest.

And then in strode Detective Aarons. "What the devil is going on?"

"That man tried to kill my niece," Aunt Butty declared, pointing an accusing finger at Carter's unconscious form.

"Worse," I croaked. "This man murdered Cyril Brumble *and* Dorothea Caron."

He rubbed his forehead as if he had a headache. "I don't suppose you can prove this."

I grinned. "Yes, actually. I can."

Chapter 17

It was some time before all the players were gathered together in Cyril's former living room. Lola's now, I supposed. First, Aunt Butty had insisted I go to the hospital to ensure Carter hadn't done any permanent damage. I'd refused to step foot in the place, so Lola had rung up her personal doctor who'd given me the all-clear.

Following police protocol, Aarons had Carter taken to the hospital to get checked out. He had a concussion, thanks to Aunt Butty, and was kept for observation under police guard. Then the police had to round up Wayne Palmer and question him to assure themselves he wasn't involved.

Naturally, while all that was going on I called Chaz and urged him to join us. I knew he wouldn't want to miss out on the excitement. "It'll help me get over my disappointment," he said.

"You didn't get the part?" I asked.

"Oh, I *did*, but Archie quit the film. Something better came along. And there's no way I'm doing this without him. Besides, I rather miss England, don't you?"

Finally, Detective Aarons arrived at the house along with a newly freed Lola. "She'd better be as innocent as you say," he warned me. There was a distinct "or else" in his tone. What was with everyone threatening me lately?

"Don't worry. She is," I said, as much to assure him as myself.

While everyone gathered in the living room, I sent Maddie away with instructions to start packing. Frankly, I couldn't wait to be shut of this place and on my way East.

Detective Aarons took up a position standing near the fireplace, his eagle eyes taking us all in. Two uniformed officers sat casually at the back of the room, occasionally sneaking a snack from the extra tea trays. Chaz sat near the French doors to the terrace, ready to pounce on anyone who might try to flee. The rest of us—Aunt Butty, myself, Lola, and Sam—sat comfortably on the sofa and chairs. Lola had been aghast when I suggested inviting Sam, but I convinced her he was part of the reason she was a free woman. She looked at him with a great deal more interest after that.

"All right, Lady R," Aarons said at last, "give us what you've got."

I cleared my throat. "Very well." My voice was still a little hoarse. "Here's what happened."

Everyone leaned forward expectantly. I smiled to myself. I did enjoy the spotlight on occasion. Can't imagine where I got that little character trait.

"Right. It was clear to me from the beginning, that despite appearances to the contrary, Cyril Brumble did not commit suicide. It was easy to see how a person might jump to that conclusion," I shot Aarons a look, "but I simply did not believe it. The problem was, of course, how to prove it."

"And did you?" Lola asked. "Prove it, I mean. For sure."

I gave her a patient smile. "Yes. I did. You see, there was no way that Cyril could have shot himself that night without anyone hearing it. The shot had to be muffled. And if that was the case, then it had to be murder. Eventually, the police came to agree with me."

Detective Aarons grimaced, but nodded in agreement.

"So, if it was murder, the question to answer next was why? Why would someone want to murder Cyril Brumble? What I found was that there were a lot of reasons. From a lot of people. First of all, there was his wife. Or rather, his ex-wife." I held up the newspaper with Dorothea Caron's face plastered on it. "She was a troubled woman, Dorothea. And although Cyril continued to help her financially, he left her for Hollywood, and eventually another woman. Did she kill him out of anger or as revenge and then throw herself from a bridge? After all, Sam heard him arguing with a woman who wasn't Lola the night he died. So was she the killer? Possible, but unlikely. You see, I saw Dorothea at the pool party. She seemed more sad than angry. So why were they arguing? Perhaps it was because he couldn't afford to pay for her anymore now that he was about to remarry. That his new wife insisted he cut the old wife off. Isn't that right, Lola?" I whirled to face Lola.

"I'd every right," she said, her face turned in a petulant frown. "It was *my* money."

"Yes, that's right. Your money. You discovered Cyril was dead broke. In fact, he had to borrow money from you at one point just to pay the bills. He owed money all over town. Even to mobsters." She glanced away, and I knew she realized I was talking about Vinnie. "Worse, you discovered that not only did Cyril have an ex-wife, but your hard-earned money was going to support her.

"But you had more than one reason to murder Cyril. He was cheating on you. And with men. Granted, you already knew about his predilections, but if it got out... well, it wouldn't be just *his* career that would be over."

Lola's face flushed red. "He was a selfish bastard. He could have ruined me. I almost wish I *had* offed him. But I didn't."

"No," I said agreeably. "You didn't. Even though it was your wrap that was used to muffle the shot that killed Cyril, you didn't fire the gun. Because you were too busy in the garage getting acrobatic with Sam." It was an absolute wild guess, but I knew I was right the moment I said it. The look on Sam's face gave it away.

Lola, on the other hand, blinked big, doe eyes at me. "I have no idea what you mean."

"Can it, doll face," Aunt Butty snapped. "I've seen the looks you two throw at each other. I doubt Sam's little crush is entirely one-sided. And I'm well aware of Cyril's proclivities. There is no way you were going to spend your married life celibate. Besides which, we're well aware of your propensity for a bit of rough." Again, the reference to Vinnie.

Lola flushed crimson but held her ground. "Don't be crass."

Chaz was beaming ear to ear, clearly enthralled by the drama. "What I need right now is popcorn," he muttered.

"Just admit it, babe," Sam said, ignoring Chaz. "We were together all night."

Lola glared. "Fine. I was with Sam."

I nodded. "Which gives him an alibi."

"Hey, I didn't have a motive for Cyril's murder," Sam said.

"Of course, you did, darling," Aunt Butty clucked. "You were fornicating with his wife. And while the dear man may have preferred the company of other men, that didn't mean he wanted his wife sleeping with the chauffeur. If he found out, you could have been fired."

"Could have," Sam admitted. "But he didn't find out."

"Of course, Dorothea herself had a perfectly good motive for killing Cyril. He left her. He married someone else. And that someone else didn't want him supporting her anymore. She had every reason to want to kill him. And she was arguing with him mere hours before his murder. She could have easily slipped back in the house later that night and shot him. Then killed herself out of remorse or despair. That is, after all, what we were supposed to think. If, that is, we didn't buy the suicide story. Isn't that right, Detective?" I asked, turning to Aarons.

He nodded. "Appears that way."

"Except there was a bit of a problem," I continued. "It was clear that the sheet of paper on which the supposed suicide note was written had been torn from a journal. Why would a suicide note be written in a journal and then torn out? Cyril was such a precise man. Very neat. He'd have written such a thing on proper stationary. So the only answer was that someone who knew him well, knew where he kept his private journal, had used that to create the impression of a suicide note. Would an ex-wife who hadn't seen her husband in years know where he kept his private journal? Likely not. Nor would she likely know where the new wife kept her clothing so as to use it to muffle the shot that killed her ex-husband.

"No, it was more likely to my mind that poor Dorothea was framed. Which left truly one person with the intimate knowledge of Cyril Brumble and his life to pull off this murder. Carter, his valet and butler."

"But why would he do that?" Lola demanded.

"Cyril and Carter had been having an affair for years," Aunt Butty supplied. "He wrote about it in his journal. Although not so specifically. Still, it was clear to the trained eye." She winked, clearly indicating her own was such an eye.

"Indeed, once you realized what he was talking about in his journals, it was pretty clear that Cyril and his valet cum butler had been very close for several years," I agreed. "But then Cyril's star began to fade, and his extravagant tastes outstretched his income. He decided to marry a woman much younger than himself. One that could support his lifestyle and hide his truth from the rest of the world."

"So what? They coulda carried on," Lola said. "I couldn't care less. As you well know, I had my own interests." She slid a look at Sam.

"True," I said. "And so they would have. Except Cyril discovered Carter's little secret. For the last several months, he's been meeting up with a much younger man. A rising star in Hollywood. Cyril considered that a betrayal. *That* was what the argument I overheard between them was about. Cyril had discovered the truth and fired Carter in a fit of jealous anger. He was a good man, though, and immediately retracted it, but he did threaten Carter should he carry on the affair. Probably as much to protect himself as anything."

"Wow," Sam muttered. "That's... wow."

"Indeed," I agreed. "Tangled webs and whatnot. Carter decided the only way out was murder. So when he overheard the argument between Dorothea and Cyril, he saw his chance. Knowing Lola was with Sam, he took her wrap and used it as a make-shift silencer, planning to leave it out where it could be found should he need to. Then he staged the scene. Put the gun in Cyril's hand, ripped a page from the journal, and so on. Finally, he hid the journal in Lola's room where she would be unlikely to look, just in case he needed a patsy."

"That's why there was a gap between his so-called discovery of the body and his phone call to the police," Aarons said.

"Yes," I confirmed. "He needed to set the stage."

"And Dorothea?" Aarons asked. There was a sparkle in his eye that told me he had a good idea where I was going with this.

"Initially, he thought he'd got away with it. The police assumed suicide. But then I had to stir things up," I admitted wryly. "Realizing Lola could, if she wanted, come up with an air tight alibi, he knew he had to frame someone else. Someone less... stable. Someone the police would never believe."

"Dorothea," Aarons said.

I nodded. "He rang her up at her hotel and asked her to meet him on the bridge. Told her that Cyril had given him some money to give to her."

"She met him, and he pushed her in the river," Aarons speculated.

"That's my guess." I smiled sadly. "Poor woman never stood a chance. He decided that if the suicide story fell flat, and Lola admitted to her alibi, there was still Dorothea."

"What a rotter that Carter is," Aunt Butty said. "Not a proper sort of butler at all. I hope they lock him up and throw away the key."

"Oh, we will," Aarons assured her.

"Jolly good show!" Chaz declared from his perch. "Better than anything on the silver screen."

Aarons eyed him narrowly. "This is real life, young man. Not some make believe story."

Chaz grinned. "Haven't you heard? All the world's a stage."

Chapter 18

"Are you sure you don't want to stay a bit longer?" Lola asked. She stood to the side of the Rolls while Maddie supervised Sam loading our luggage into the back of a taxi. The way he was huffing and puffing and sweating, I half feared he'd keel over from heat exhaustion.

"That's very kind of you," Aunt Butty said, patting her hand. "But we're meeting Chaz at the train station and we've an ocean liner to catch in New York. Ophelia's very keen on a trip to her villa in the south of France." She gave me a knowing wink which I ignored. I did not want to discuss my involvement with Hale in front of Lola.

I walked over to the car to see if I could help, but Sam had everything under control.

"Will you stay on here?" I asked Sam softly, out of Lola's hearing.

He gave me a one shoulder shrug as he glanced over at the woman in question. "For now."

"You know she'll ditch you for the next man that comes along who can get her the right part or the top billing?" That was Lola's way. My guess was she'd been with Vinnie because he had connections. I knew she'd been with Cyril for the same reason. It had worked for her then, and it would no doubt work for her in the future.

"Yeah, I know," he admitted. "But for now, well, I'll take what I can get."

I nodded. Silly man. Still, he knew what he was getting into.

As we drove down the drive, following the taxi carrying Maddie and the luggage, Aunt Butty and I waved to Lola until she was out of sight. Then we settled in comfortably for the trip to the train station.

"That was... more adventurous than expected," I said finally.

"One for the memoirs, I suppose," Aunt Butty mused. "Though I doubt anyone who wasn't there will ever believe it."

"What do you suppose will happen to Lola?"

"As you said, no doubt she'll find another man to hitch her star to. One that will help her rise further. Overcome her great loss." Her tone was just this side of sarcastic at that last bit. "I've known women like her my whole life. Can't stand on their own two feet, so they rope in whatever man to do it for them. Cyril was a miscalculation on her part. No doubt one she won't repeat. But at least she has promised to get Vernon a role as an extra on her next movie," Aunt Butty said smugly.

"The kid from the hotel? How'd you manage that?" I asked.

"Oh, I have my ways. Never let it be said I went back on my word."

"Never, indeed."

Aunt Butty folded her hands neatly in her lap. "Now for some *real* relaxation. No more adventures for the time being."

"No more adventures," I agreed. "My villa will be perfect. Nothing ever happens there." A green Duesenberg suddenly passed us on the left, and I leaned forward. "Wait! Is that Gary Cooper?"

"I believe it is," Sam called from the front.

I sighed. "That man is so handsome it should be illegal."

Aunt Butty pressed her face against the glass. "And I never even got his autograph!"

Keep reading for a sample of Lady Rample's next adventure:

Lady Rample Sits In

Chapter 1

"We're all going to die."

The words were spoken with such grim finality that one might find oneself believing them if not for the fact they were spoken by my maid, Maddie. While not prone to histrionics generally, she did tend to look on the not-so-bright side of things. And as the sea was currently calm as glass, one could be fairly certain she was exaggerating.

"We're not going to die, Maddie," my Aunt Butty said bracingly as she strode down the deck of the *Ile de France*—possibly the most beautiful ocean liner I'd ever seen.

"We are so, M'lady," Maddie insisted with great stubbornness, trotting after her. "People weren't meant to travel like this. We'll sink to the bottom for sure."

"Nonsense," I said. "You had no problems on the outbound journey." She hadn't even gotten seasick, which was more than I could say for myself. The voyage from England to America had been uneventful for everyone in our party but myself. I'd spent a great deal of time in my room.

"That were on a bigger boat," Maddie pointed out. "This thing could get tossed about easy. One gust of wind and we're in Davy Jones's locker!"

"This is a perfectly sound vessel. Not the fastest, but quite glamorous. And we'll be in Le Havre in seven days. I, for one, look forward to the voyage." Aunt Butty adjusted her hat—a bright orange monstrosity festooned with garish yellow ribbons and peacock feathers dyed vermillion. More than a few passengers stared, but Aunt Butty ignored them utterly. In another time, she might have been called An Original. As it was, I was beginning to think she might be color blind.

"Come, Ophelia," she called to me. "Let's take a turn about the deck. Maddie, don't dawdle."

I followed in Aunt Butty's wake, Maddie bringing up the rear clutching a massive carpet bag to her flat chest. Within it were the accoutrements Aunt Butty insisted on having with her at all times. I'd no idea what was in there, but I felt sorry for Maddie. It looked heavy.

We'd left Hollywood eleven days earlier and none too soon for my tastes. Yes, it was glamorous, but it was also exhausting and rather...well, fake, if I were honest. And then there was that ghastly murder business and being kidnapped by gangsters...I'd be very glad to get my feet back on English soil.

Except, I reminded myself, we weren't headed to England, but to Le Havre, France where we would then catch a train to Nice and my villa. And I would finally be able to see Hale Davis—my paramour, for lack of a better word—again. Too bad Aunt Butty had insisted on opulence over speed in choosing a mode of transportation or I could have seen him a few days earlier. Alas, Aunt Butty had a way of getting what she wanted. And so we set sail from New York on the *Ile de France* with all the pomp and circumstance due our station.

My name is Ophelia, Lady Rample, widow of the late Lord Rample. Thanks to his generosity I'm richer than a person has any right to be and absolutely free to do as I please, when I please. A fact which stirred up the upper crust into a veritable tizzy. They did not approve, and yet there wasn't a thing they could do about it. Which amused me no end. Sometimes I was more like my aunt than I might want to admit.

She was my mother's sister and had done very well herself in the marriage department. More than once, if I were honest. She lived exactly how she liked with no care as to what anyone else thought. Quite Bohemian, really. Also, she had ghastly taste in hats.

"Have you seen Chaz, Aunt Butty?" Chaz was my best friend and sometime sleuthing partner. He'd been visiting a friend out in Hollywood at the same time we were there for a wedding. After the exhausting events that ensued, I'd invited him to join us at my villa and we'd all decided to take the same ship together.

"Haven't seen him since we boarded. I'm sure he's about. No doubt in the smoking parlor playing cards with the other young men."

"No doubt," I murmured. Chaz did enjoy a good game. And the occasional young man.

"We're dining at the Captain's table tonight," Aunt Butty announced out of nowhere.

"Yes, Aunt, I'm aware." It was apparently a great honor to dine at the Captain's table. Frankly, I doubted there would be anyone interesting there. Just a lot of stuffy people with too much money and not enough sense. Which was a little like the pot and the kettle except that I certainly had some sense. I had, after all, not been born wealthy and had instead been raised by a vicar. So, maybe not so much sense after all.

"What do you plan to wear? I thought I'd wear that pink number I picked up in New York."

I managed to hold back a horrified gasp. The "pink number" was a rather lovely bias-cut gown in a satin fabric that was absolutely destroyed by being flamingo pink and having layers of ruffled tiers flowing from the waistline, making my aunt's hips and backside look even more voluptuous than they already were. Worse, she'd the habit of pairing it with an equally pink bolero jacket trimmed in black ostrich feathers.

"The Coco," I replied quickly. The stunning blue gown had only been worn once in Hollywood. I doubted there would be anyone here to see that I wore it again. Beside which, it was too delicious to leave lying in a steamer trunk. Unlike some women of my class who insisted on never wearing a gown twice, I bought dressed because I liked them and wished to wear them often. I considered wearing a dress once to be a waste of good money.

"Excellent choice," Aunt Butty approved. "Oh, look. There are the Whatsits. I must go say hello. I'll see you at dinner, Ophelia." And she sailed off without a backward glance, leaving poor Maddie looking confused.

"You better go after her," I said. "Just in case she needs anything."

Maddie rolled her eyes. "Miss Butty—"

"Lady Lucas," I correct.

She sighed heavily. "Lady Lucas probably forgot I was even here."

No doubt she was right, but I shooed her off anyway. Maddie might be my maid, but she was doing for both Aunt Butty and me this trip, plus I could use a bit of time to myself.

It had been a long and tiring journey from the West Coast of the States and a nap sounded just the thing. There was plenty of time before dinner, and I wanted to feel my best.

As I made my way toward my stateroom, I took a corner a little too sharply and barreled into someone. I careened backward into a bulkhead and barely caught myself.

"Oh, I say!" The tone was male and outraged.

"So sorry," I said, glancing down. It wasn't often I was forced to look down, but the man who I had crashed into was barely shoulder height, round as a billiard ball, and cherubic of face, though he must be long past sixty. He looked like a very scowly Father Christmas.

He let out a huff, straightened his jacket, and marched off without a word. Dashed rude if you ask me.

Recovering my wits, I continued on to my room, but the memory of that angry Father Christmas face stayed with me.

The first-class dining room was a massive, rectangular space well-lit by dozens of small, square lighting fixtures set flush in the ceiling and decorated in gray marble and gold accents. All very art deco. At one end, a mural of a water fall stretched nearly three decks high. On the other end, an elegant staircase. In the middle of the room stood a sculptural fountain of light spires shooting up from a wide chrome bowl.

"This is the largest dining room afloat, did you know?" Aunt Butty said, leading the way in.

"Er, no, I didn't."

"Ladies." The black-garbed maître d' stepped forward. "If you will please follow me to the Captain's table."

"Lead on," Aunt Butty ordered airily. I held back a smirk.

The man led us through the tables toward the head table. As we passed by the fountain, I noticed the round man I'd bumped into earlier seated next to a plump, gray-haired woman in a frothy peach dress much too young for her.

"Excuse me," I said to the maître d'. "Who is that couple over there?"

The maître d' slid a side-ways glance at the couple. "Ah. That is Sir Eustace Scrubbs and his wife, Lady Scrubbs."

"Thank you." I had never heard of Sir Eustace Scrubbs or his wife, nor had I seen them at any society functions. I determined to ask Aunt Butty about them when we had a moment to ourselves. I couldn't say why I was so curious, but I was. Something just felt a bit off about Sir Eustace.

At last we arrived to be greeted by Captain Blancart who introduced us around the table. "Perhaps you know the Comtesse de Angouleme."

Aunt Butty gave the older woman a stiff nod. "Antonia."

The Comtesse sniffed. "Mrs. Trent."

Aunt Butty's eyes narrowed and I was half afraid there'd be a brawl right then and there. Although Aunt Butty's most recent husband had been a mere Mr. Trent, she preferred going by her second husband's name—or was it third?—Lady Lucas. Fortunately, the Captain, being a man of vast intelligence, quickly moved on. "Mr. Virgil Brightwell and his son, Mr. Alexander Brightwell, hailing from Texas."

"How do, ladies?" Mr. Alexander Brightwell was around Aunt Butty's age, dressed in a western style suit with a string bowtie. I'd bet anything he had cowboy boots on under the table. His son was a few years younger than myself, and dressed with a great deal less...character.

"Mrs. Verity Jones," he said, turning to a handsome, middle-aged woman dressed almost as colorfully as Aunt Butty. Both her name and face seemed familiar, but I couldn't place either.

"Charmed," Mrs. Jones said with broad smile.

"And finally," the Captain turned to the young couple at the table, "Mr. and Mrs. Geisel from New York. We're still waiting for our final guest."

Mr. Geisel had thick, black eyebrows and a rather prominent nose. Mrs. Geisel had short, dark hair and a wide smile. I was seated next to her, with Aunt Butty seated next to Mr. Geisel.

"I'm sorry," Mrs. Geisel said softy, "but I take it Mrs. Trent isn't your name?"

"I prefer Lady Lucas," Aunt Butty said. "But you can call me Butty. Everyone does."

"And I'm Helen," Mrs. Geisel offered.

"I prefer to be called 'Dr. Seuss,'" Mr. Geisel said.

Aunt Butty frowned. "Zeus? Like the Greek god? Oh, I love Greece. When I was in my twenties I met this gorgeous Greek man—"

"No, Aunt Butty," I interrupted whatever inappropriate story she was about to launch into. "It's 'Sousa' — like the American composer."

Dr. Seuss grimaced. "No, no... just Seuss."

Aunt Butty laughed. "Oh, we must seem like children who need you to spell that out for us with pictures."

"Funny you should say that," Helen said. "Theodor is quite the artist. I've been telling him he should write a children's book."

"I draw cartoons, dear," he said dryly.

"Still, that's very artistic," Aunt Butty said generously. "I couldn't draw a straight line to save my life!"

"Are you travelling to France?" I asked Helen.

"Of course, they're travelling to France, Ophelia," Aunt Butty laughed. "We're *all* travelling to France."

I rolled my eyes. "I mean, what is your final stop?"

Helen grinned. "We're going to travel all over France. That's the plan, isn't it, Theodor? We adore exploring new countries."

"Yes, dear," Dr. Seuss agreed. "We've been to, what? A dozen so far?"

"I'd have to count, but something like that," Helen agreed. "I can't wait to drink real French wine in a real French vineyard!"

Just then Chaz arrived, looking dapper in a black tux, his dark hair sleeked back. The Captain introduced him around as our final diner, which came as a pleasant surprise. He hadn't told me he'd be dinging at the Captain's table with us. He gave me a little wave from where he was seated down between the Comtesse and Mrs. Jones.

While Aunt Butty and Helen espoused the virtues of French wine versus Italian wine with Mrs. Geisel, I took a moment to address Mr. Alexander Brightwell, who was seated on my left. He was a reasonably handsome young man in a bland, pasty sort of way, as if the colorfulness of the father had been leached right out of the son, leaving behind a shadow. A pale imitation.

"So, you're from Texas?" I asked.

"Yes. My father has a small ranch there."

My guess was that as he was sailing on the *Ile de France* and seated at the Captain's table, it was more than a small ranch. "Do you work there also? On the ranch, I mean?"

He didn't look the sort. His skin was too pale, his suit too neat, and his hands too soft. Unlike his father who was hearty, tanned, and rough around the edges.

"Oh, no, my father wanted me to do something more with my life. I just finished my law degree. And before I sit for the bar exam, my father decided I needed a little reward. Hence this trip to Europe." He didn't seem excited.

Frankly, I'd have given my eyeteeth for a chance to tour Europe, but my father wasn't the sort to do such a thing, even if he'd had the money. And even though Aunt Butty had and would have gladly taken me wherever I wished to go, by the time she'd rescued me from a life of drudgery at the vicarage, it wasn't long before we were at war and travel was no longer an option.

Since I doubted the younger Mr. Brightwell would appreciate a lecture from me on thankfulness, I murmured something vague and then turned my attention elsewhere. People watching was a favored pastime of mine. I find them so fascinating. What makes them tick? Why does one person end up with another? My mother used to say I had an overactive imagination. I don't think there's any such thing.

From where I sat, I couldn't see Sir Eustace or his wife. The fountain stood in the way. Too bad. It would have been interesting to see how the angry little man got on with his wife. She'd looked frightfully out of place in her too-young gown. Not at all the sort I'd expect to be married to a knight. Perhaps he gained his knighthood late in life and came from a common background. That would explain her lack of taste. Then again, he'd sounded posh enough. Perhaps a third son of a third son or the like.

Curiosity or no, I didn't want my trip spoiled by Sir Eustace's unpleasantness, so I determined to avoid the man at all costs and put him promptly out of my head. I didn't think about him again for the entirety of the voyage. Although I might have done differently if I'd known what was to come.

Coming Fall of 2018

Lady Rample Sits In

Lady Rample Mysteries - Book Four

Sign up for updates on Lady Rample:
https://www.subscribepage.com/cozymystery

Note from the Author

Thank you for reading. If you enjoyed this book, I'd appreciate it if you'd help others find it so they can enjoy it too.

- Review it: Let other potential readers know what you liked or didn't like about the story.

- Sign Up: Join in on the fun on Shéa's email list: https://www.subscribepage.com/cozymystery

Book updates can be found at www.sheamacleod.com

About Shéa MacLeod

Shéa MacLeod is the author of the bestselling paranormal series, Sunwalker Saga, as well as the award nominated cozy mystery series Viola Roberts Cozy Mysteries. She has dreamed of writing novels since before she could hold a crayon. She totally blames her mother.

She resides in the leafy green hills outside Portland, Oregon where she indulges in her fondness for strong coffee, Ancient Aliens reruns, lemon curd, and dragons. She can usually be found at her desk dreaming of ways to kill people (or vampires). Fictionally speaking, of course.

Other books by Shéa MacLeod

Lady Rample Mysteries
Lady Rample Steps Out
Lady Rample Spies a Clue
Lady Rample and the Silver Screen
Lady Rample Sits In (Coming Autumn 2018)

Viola Roberts Cozy Mysteries
The Corpse in the Cabana
The Stiff in the Study
The Poison in the Pudding
The Body in the Bathtub
The Venom in the Valentine
The Remains in the Rectory
The Death in the Drink

Notting Hill Diaries
To Kiss A Prince
Kissing Frogs
Kiss Me, Chloe
Kiss Me, Stupid
Kissing Mr. Darcy

<u>Sunwalker Saga: Soulshifter Trilogy</u>

Fearless

Haunted

Soulshifter

<u>Sunwalker Saga: Witchblood</u>

Spellwalker

Deathwalker

Mistwalker

<u>Omicron ZX</u>

Omicron Zed-X

A Rage of Angels

CPSIA information can be obtained
at www.ICGtesting.com
Printed in the USA
LVHW092134310319
612496LV00001B/149/P